The Messenger

The Messenger

Dr. Seema Bajaj

MOONLIGHT BOOKS

THE MESSENGER

FIRST EDITION: 2020

ISBN PB: 978-81-940809-6-1
ISBN EBOOK: 978-81-940809-7-8

Published by

MOONLIGHT BOOKS
20 Ekjot Apartment, Pitampura, Delhi-110034, India
Email: moonlightbooks2016@gmail.com
www.moonlightbooks.in

Repro Books Limited, Mumbai

Foreword

'The Messenger' is a work of historical fiction set in the mid sixteenth century Agra. It pays attention to the manner, social conditions and other details of the period depicted and tries to be as accurate as possible with dates and other historical events. The historical characters of Maharana Pratap, Emperor Akbar, Queen Heera Kunwari (Jodha Bai), Raja Todar Mal and Maham Anga are real; but the other characters of the story are fictitious and events invented.

Dr. Seema Bajaj

Contents

Foreword — *v*

1 Radha 1566 AD Agra — 01
2 Suraj — 07
3 The Emperor — 12
4 Agra Bazaar — 17
5 Murder in the Market Place — 23
6 A Sleepless Night — 28
7 The Emperor's Hunt — 34
8. The Secret — 40
9 By the Banks of the Yamuna — 45
10 A Discreet Meeting — 51
11 Radha's Dilemma — 56
12 Assad Khan Investigates — 63
13 Radha's Plans — 70
14 The Sarai — 75
15 Radha in the Fort — 80
16 The Adventure in the Fort — 86
17 An Evening of Suspense — 93
18 The Interview — 100

19 An Eventful Day 107
20 Another Sleepless Night 111
21 Another Murder 115
22 Assad Khan Meets the Emperor 120
23 A Much Awaited Meeting 125
24 Suraj's Narrative 129
25 Assad Khan's Narrative 134
26 Face-off 138
27 The Long Goodbye 142
Glossary 148

One

RADHA

1566 AD AGRA

It was the month of June in the eleventh year of the reign of Emperor Akbar. The sun had reached the western sky but it was still hot. People were inside their homes waiting for the sun to set. Agra, the city which Jalaluddin Mohammad had decided to make his capital, had been baking all afternoon in the summer sun. Agra, the city where Jalaluddin's grandfather Babar had first set out to rule Hindustan from the Agra fort. The city on the banks of the mighty Yamuna. The city which had witnessed his tumultuous growing years after his father Humayun's early death.

It was in this city, on a lazy summer afternoon, that a young girl called Radha waited restlessly for the cool of the evening to set in. The heat of the afternoon had kept people inside the shelters of their homes. Evenings were eagerly awaited and Radha was waiting to go out with her best friend Gauri. The gentle snoring of her mother in the next room made her feel restless to go outside. Her mother would never miss her afternoon nap and Radha could never get herself to sleep in the day. Gauri was late. It was just like Gauri to be late for everything. Childhood habits never change, thought Radha, and neither do childhood friendships.

Radha decided to bide her time by finishing the painting she had started a week ago.

Her father Bihari Mal was an officer in Raja Todar Mal's office. The past few months he had been out of town on business with Raja Todar Mal and a few other officers.

She was busy with the painting of Krishna herding his cows, when her friend Gauri called. Gauri was the same age as Radha. But while Gauri was fairer, Radha was taller. Their beauty was in their simplicity and of course their youth. Youth has a beauty which is original and captivating. A beauty when seen through the eyes of the older ones makes them regret its impermanence. The two friends fell into deep conversation and soon were oblivious to time.

The 'Haveli' where Radha lived with her family was spacious. It had been built by her great-grandfather and was simple in style. It's many rooms opened into the courtyard. The kitchen and the bathrooms among the other rooms were on the ground floor. Radha had a room on the first floor. Her younger brothers also had their rooms there, but they were away in a Gurukul near Delhi for their higher schooling. Radha and Gauri were sitting by the window in her room. Gauri was getting married after a month and she always had some stories to tell about her husband to be Baldev. He was a Zamindar's son and lived in a village not very far from Agra. He owned a lot of land. Today Gauri was excited about the jewelry her father was getting made for her from a famous goldsmith in the city. Radha listened patiently to Gauri's chatter. She observed the changing hues of the sky from her window. Soon, the sun, already low in the western sky, would start changing colors and become a huge orange ball. And then, before you could even comprehend the daily wonder, the great ball descended into the horizon. Radha wondered where it rested before coming up again the next day. Her tutor had never explained it satisfactorily. Her mother, Janki, came to their room with sweets for them. How fond her mother was of making sweets!

"Gauri, how is your mother ? Are you helping her with the wedding preparations or just nagging her with your demands?"

"No, Mausi, I never trouble Maa," Gauri retorted quickly.

"Now that you will be leaving her soon, try to make most of the time that you have with her," said Janki.

Janki sighed and got up. Radha sensed that her mother's thoughts were preoccupied with her marriage. Janki went down to light the evening lamp in the beautiful little temple they had in their haveli. Janki's native village was near Mathura and she was a devout follower of Krishna. She had named her sons Brijmohan and Gopal. Life was beginning to be a little peaceful in the Badshah's reign. His lifting of Jazia had lifted a big burden off the Hindus. They were no longer afraid of being seen offering prayers and performing their rituals.

Radha was not as ritualistic as her mother though she liked to join her in the evening prayers.

After a while her mother came up to her room again to light the evening lamp. She would then go to the little temple inside the Haveli to perform her evening prayers. Lata, her mother's daily help was preparing dinner. Her husband Magan Lal was a cook in the Royal kitchen and they lived in quarters inside the fort. The fort was close to the haveli. Lata spent most of her waking hours here with Radha and her mother.

"Amma, dinner is ready. Eat it while it's hot", shouted Lata.

She had entered their household when she was just twelve years old and after twenty years she was like another daughter of the house.

"Amma, can I go to Gauri's house after dinner?", asked Radha.

"Why, it's so late?" asked her mother.

"She wants to show me her new sarees that her father has got from Kashi."

"Not so late Radha," said her mother, "you can go in the morning." Radha knew her mother would not let her go at night. She bade Gauri goodbye.

Sleep was still in a far away land. Radha was reluctant to call it a day so soon.

She thought of completing the painting by candle light till sleep came. She had been fascinated by the colors of the sky at sunset today and had observed them closely. She decided to use that as a background in her painting of Krishna, the cowherd, bringing his cows back home at dusk.

Since her father and brothers were away from home, their man servant Mukundi, slept inside the haveli to keep guard. He always locked the main door and surveyed the haveli with a mashaal before going to sleep in the courtyard. He performed the same ritual tonight. Finally he placed the mashaal in its niche in the wall and went off to sleep.

The folk of Agra had retired from the day's work. Some were home, seeking the comfort of their families, while others sought comfort in the company of friends and liquor. The nobility preferred to revel in the company of beautiful dancer girls while their wives sought comfort elsewhere. While most of Agra slept, a stranger to the city ran for his life.

It was difficult finding his way in a strange city,

especially at night and especially when being chased. Suraj knew he did not have the option of getting caught. Being caught meant death, either at his own hands or at the hands of the enemy. He ran as fast as he could, keeping ahead of them. The moon light was helping him, but it would be helping the enemy too. And they knew the streets of Agra like he knew the streets of Ajmer.

He was out of breath now and needed a few moments to slow down his breath and calm down his heart. He dared a quick glance behind. No one was in sight. No footsteps echoed in the silence of the night. He looked up and saw an open window.

✪✪✪✪✪✪

Two

SURAJ

The Sun had risen and with it had risen its most faithful followers, the birds. People followed soon. The darkness of the night, which had covered the private lives of people, now gave way to the light of the sun, and people crawled out of their beds to start another day. Radha turned to her side. It was time to get up. The early morning aura filled her room. The sweet chirping sounds of the birds, the soothing rays of the morning sun streaming through her window, the hurried footsteps of Lata in the courtyard; and Radha could no longer close her eyes.

Their household followed the routine of early to bed and early to rise. She sat up in her the bed and thought of completing her painting today. Her father was also expected to come back in a day or two. She was still sitting in bed and knotting her loose hair when she heard the rhythmic sound of someone breathing. She froze, thinking that some animal had entered her room at night. The very next moment she looked about the room and gasped loudly. A strange man slept peacefully at the other end of the room. How did it happen? Who was he? When did he enter the room? Why did she not hear a sound? Should she awaken him or call her mother? So many thoughts were racing through her mind while she continued to sit in her bed, looking at the stranger who was sleeping in her room, without her awareness or her permission.

As though he felt her gaze or heard her questions, Suraj woke up. Perhaps he was more astonished to see Radha than she was on discovering him. When he had taken shelter in the room last night, he had been too exhausted to look out for anyone in the room. The room had been dark and quiet and he had presumed that it was empty. His surprise on seeing a beautiful, young girl sitting before him was no less than Radha's on finding him in her room. For a long moment he could not take his eyes off the young girl who was by now staring hard at him. His senses had been dulled by sleep and lack of food. He could not think of how to explain his presence in the room.

His reverie broke when Radha gave a low cry on seeing his blood stained tunic. The blood had seeped to the floor and stained it. Radha opened her mouth to speak, but the stranger got up with a jerk. He was tall and sharp featured. “Is he a Mughal? Why has he spent the night in my room?”, thought Radha. She was about to speak up, but he cut her short again by speaking before she could question him. “I am sorry to have intruded your privacy. Last night I was being chased by some thugs and the first escape visible to me was your open window. I was injured and exhausted by the time I reached your house and the temptation of an open window and a tree next to it was too much to resist. That is all I can tell you in my defense and would request you to keep this incident to yourself,” Suraj blurted out in the form of an explanation.

He wanted to leave before the girl with the large inquisitive eyes started to ask him questions or raised an alarm. Radha hardly had time to comprehend what he said or to collect her senses, that the stranger looked down the window and disappeared from her view.

She ran to the window only to see him looking up with a finger on his lips and not hardly a grateful look in his eyes.

Radha’s curiosity and fear now gave way to anger. How could he go away without even letting her speak, not to mention about thanking her. He was rather ordering her into silence about the whole incident. She turned back to her room. She saw the blood stains on the floor and her temper rose higher. How did he imagine her to clean the blood stains off the floor without arousing her mother’s or Lata’s suspicion? Radha had been blessed with a happy and cheerful nature. She did not feel her own self if she stayed angry for long.

She decided to clean the floor before Lata or her mother noticed it. It was going to be difficult but she would manage and it would avoid a lot of explanations. Besides, the stranger wanted the incident to be kept a secret, so it would be for the present. She ran down with stealthy feet and came back quickly with a bucket of water and a mop.

While scrubbing the floor, her thoughts kept returning to him. Her kind-heartedness made her worry about his wound. His spending the night in her room meant he had no good friends to turn to for help. Was he injured badly? She could have dressed his wound had he given her the time. She was excited about what had happened and wanted to talk to someone about the incident. She thought of going to Gauri's house, but then decided against it. There was little chance that the stranger's entry into their house would be of any significance or that she would meet him again. On the other hand if her parents came to know about it they would start worrying. Her mother would insist that she shut her window at night. Radha always kept her window open to feel the cool summer breeze at night. Few sparrows had made nests in the old mango tree next to the window. Radha loved their soft chirps and frenzy of activity at dawn and dusk. She decided that it was best to remain silent. That would fulfill the stranger's wish also, she thought and smiled.

While Radha's thoughts dwelt on him, a hungry and wounded Suraj was not completely in control of himself. He had impulsively left the girl's room and now he was regretting it. A glass or two of water before leaving would have helped. The thirst and hunger made him irritable and he cursed himself as he always liked to be in control of situations. His plan was definitely not going as desired. The chase yesterday had made him desperate to look for cover. When he had entered the room last night, he was sure it was vacant. He had failed to notice the girl sleeping in the room. He had failed to notice the bed itself due to his extreme exhaustion and had fallen asleep as soon as he had laid his head on the floor.

It was difficult to forget those dark brown eyes as they stared at him and talked their own language. She was hardly frightened of him, which was odd. She looked more angry for his leaving without any explanation. He chuckled to himself. Serves her right for looking so beautiful early in the morning, he thought. Right now all he needed was some food and a place to inspect his wound. He would have to take a risk and meet his secret contact in Agra after all. He could not roam the streets of Agra in this state and there was a chance the wound might get infected. It was a roadblock early in the mission. He cursed himself again for allowing them to wound him. He should have been more cautious. After all the enemy was known for his ruthlessness.

✪✪✪✪✪✪

Three

THE EMPEROR

Abu Fateh Jalaluddin Mohammad Akbar, all of two decades and four years, in his full regalia, was in a meeting with his ministers in the Diwaane Khaas. The mid -June heat was starting to get oppressive. The monsoon clouds approaching Northern India from down south were eagerly awaited, both by the nobles and the commoners. The monsoons would pour equally for all.

Today's meeting was with one the officers of his able finance minister Todar Mal. Raja Todar Mal was busy touring a few nearby villages and meeting the peasants who cultivated land there. The zabt or land revenue collection system was still irregular. The farming of land being entirely dependant on the rains, the produce was variable every year. Todar Mal was working on a standardised revenue collection system. This was the chief agenda of today's meeting. Last year, monsoons had betrayed the land, leaving the farmers penniless. A good one was expected this year. What weighed on the Emperor's mind though was not zabt. He knew the very efficient Todar Mal would work out a meticulous system.

It was Mewar, the garden of Rajasthan where his thoughts dwelt. His dream of bringing the entire Rajputana under his empire would be far from complete without Mewar. It's present ruler Rana Udai Singh was not a very strong man, but his son Pratap was a man of extra-ordinary stature. News had reached him through his spies that he was perpetually preparing for war against the Mughals. He disdained the Rajputs who had accepted the scepter of the Mughals.

"Neither does he live in peace nor does he let me," the Emperor was thinking. He was contemplating of sending another emissary before considering war as an option. He sighed. The empire would be incomplete without the fort of Chittor to decorate it.

Meanwhile, Todar Mal's subordinate had outlined his plan in complete detail. He had worked on it well but for the Emperor the sheets of paper and their calculations held no significance. The written words on the sheets were no different to him as those written in any other book or paper. He was an illiterate. A dyslexic since childhood, he had avoided all his teachers to such an extent that they finally had to give up on him. What he could not read, he covered up amply, by hearing about it with attention to the minutest detail. He had heard enough of the new revenue method to give his consent.

He dismissed the court and sent for Assad Khan, the Chief of the Royal secret service.

"What news of Pratap?" he asked.

Assad Khan, a lean and tall man of about fifty, saluted the Emperor before answering.

"It is very difficult to know what goes on in his mind Sir", replied Assad Khan. "The latest information we have is of his increasing friendship with the Bhil tribe in the forest. It is stronger than his alliance with all the other Rajputs. There is a rumor that he is learning their warfare."

The Emperor had not expected this and the humid air suddenly became more oppressive. Sensing his discomfort the fan bearers started moving the air faster. He asked for some water. He always drank the water of the Ganges, after boiling it and nothing else.

The stubbornness of Mewar to concede to the Mughal Empire was now a matter of Mughal pride. It was getting personal between him and Pratap Singh. He knew it was not Rana Udai Singh but his son Pratap that he was up against.

Perhaps, Bhagwan Das, would be able to make him see the light. Bhagwan Das, the prince of Amer and the Emperor's brother-in-law was away in Bengal at present.

He ordered a messenger to be sent to Bengal at once to call him back.

Surya pratap Singh, warrior par excellence, was born in the city of Ajmer. His father Rudra Pratap Singh was a commander in Rana Udai Singh's army. He had been one of the Chief instructors of Pratap Singh, the Rana's eldest son. His son, Surya Pratap, called Suraj by his friends was a couple of years younger than Pratap. He had been trained very strictly and diligently, right from his early childhood, in sword fight and horse riding. When Suraj came of age, he joined the army in the footsteps of his father, and was already popular due his extraordinary fighting skills. His expertise in horse riding had brought him in the notice of Pratap who was a connoisseur of horses. Pratap was the prince in waiting to the illustrious house of Mewar. The Emperor Jalaluddin's ambition of bringing the whole of Rajputana under the Mughal flag was a constant sore for Pratap. The marriages of convenience with the Mughals, that were becoming a rule rather than an exception, were anathema to him. He abhorred the idea of kneeling before the Mughals. Twenty six years of age, just two years older than the Mughal Emperor, he was almost seven feet tall. He loved his independence and Mewar more than his life.

He was instinctively drawn towards Surya Pratap Singh, the commander's son as he sensed the same patriotism in him. Suraj, on his part revered the prince. They often practiced their swords together and raced their horses.

It was on one such day, when Suraj had won the race and their horses were trotting back to the palace, that Pratap broached the issue. He had a mission for Suraj. It was a sensitive and dangerous one and so he trusted only Suraj for the job. Suraj was hesitant at first, because to do something surreptitiously was unlike him. Pratap however convinced him of the vile and ruthless nature of the enemy and he relented. That was at least five or six full moons back.

Now, here he was, the mighty Suraj, Pratap's bosom pal, injured in the midst of Agra, looking for something to eat. He bought a few bananas and sat in a quiet place. His thoughts were scattered and lacked clarity. He needed to plan and act fast. His biggest drawback was that Agra and it's people were unknown to him. He asked a passer by for a well and started to walk towards it. He had just walked a few metres when he sensed that he was being followed. He had no intention of looking back and decided to turn in a narrow by-lane. The sound of feet following him echoed in the deserted street. He continued at an unhurried pace and stopped abruptly at the turn where the narrow by-lane merged with a broader street. The man following continued to walk, turned in the direction of the street and with a hesitant step walked past him. Suraj immediately turned back into the deserted by-lane and waited there, well hidden from the view of others. The sound of footsteps soon died away. He sighed; he had never thought while leaving home that his stay in Agra would be so unpredictable and adventurous.

✪✪✪✪✪✪

Four

AGRA BAZAAR

Radha's house was resonating with the early morning activities. Mukundi had brought in fresh milk after milking their cow. It was his duty to milk the cows in their backyard every morning. Radha's mother was busy with preparations for her morning prayers. Lata was engaged in the kitchen. Radha, tired after rubbing the blood stain off the floor, was looking for an appropriate time to dispose off the water and the mop, and to keep the bucket back to where it belonged. Lata was putting the milk on boil. Radha quietly put the bucket back in place and ran back to her room.

"Radha, what are you doing in your room? It's so late. Come down and take a bath", her mother shouted from the prayer room.

"Coming Maa!", Radha shouted back. She hurried down. After performing her daily ablutions she had her breakfast of milk and porridge. She went back to her room to resume her painting. She had hardly started that she felt restless again. She felt angry and excited at the same time, as if someone she knew had come into her life and left all of a sudden, without answering her questions. She took up her painting again but the colors had almost finished. She would have to go to the market and buy some blue color for her painting.

She went down and took some coins from her mother to buy the color.

"Don't take too long in the market; and why is your hair so untidy today? Come, let me braid it for you."

"It's fine Maa. I just combed it", Radha replied.

Without giving heed to Radha, her mother forced her to sit and combed and braided her long hair. She took some more coins from the money box and gave it to her." "Get some sandal wood for my Krishna", her mother said. Radha nodded and sprinted across the courtyard before her mother had something more to say.

When Radha reached the market place, the fruit and vegetable vendors were busy with their customers, but the other shops were yet to start business. Fortunately, the owner of the shop which sold the colors had just arrived and Radha waited outside his shop.

It was then, that all of a sudden, as if in a dream, the stranger from last night walked right past her. He was in a hurry but he must have sensed her presence because he stopped abruptly and looked back at her. The same eyes, the same look. Radha took a step forward, but as if eager to avoid her he walked away fast.

"Radha, have your colours finished again?", said the shopkeeper. Radha came back from her reverie. "Give me some blue color. The rest I have", she said, her eyes still following the back of the stranger till he disappeared from her sight.

She paid for the color and sauntered towards the shop that sold sandal wood. It was still shut. She decided to wait. She was thinking about the suddenness of meeting the stranger again when she heard a commotion in the market. People were rushing towards a corner of the market place. Radha's curiosity got the better of her and she walked towards the crowd. A few women who had come to buy vegetables were standing away from the crowd and talking in whispers.

"What is the matter?" asked Radha.

"Looks like a man is lying dead in the next street. Slit right across the neck. By the look of the blood he must have been killed not long back", one lady spoke up.

"Who was he?", Radha asked one of the women.

"No one knows yet. They are saying he looks like a Mughal from his attire."

The thought of a man lying dead, murdered in the next street, made Radha anxious. She forgot about the sandal wood and hurried back.

The market was abuzz. The news of any murder spreads faster than fire. It is human nature to always show greater concern in matters unrelated to them. People stood in groups discussing the death solemnly. Everyone had a different opinion about the possible reason for murder. Someone had enough presence of mind to inform the Kotwal.

The Kotwal arrived after some time, mounted on a magnificent black horse with two of his subordinates behind him. The crowd made way for his horse. A short, stocky man of middle age, he dismounted the horse rubbing his eyes. The look on his face was of one aroused forcibly from a deep slumber. His hunger had made him irritable. He was in a hurry to wrap up the investigation as fast as possible and go back to his Kotwali. He looked around for some food but all he could see were fresh fruits and vegetables.

"Move aside everyone", he growled as if trying to drown the grumblings of his empty stomach. "Who has such a bad sense of timing to be murdered at this early hour when half of Agra is yet to rise from their drunken stupor", he was thinking.

"Move aside, get back to your work, you idle fellows. Have you never seen a dead man?", he said aloud. People began to move away reluctantly but loitered around with the hope of catching some piece of information.

"Who discovered the body?", the Kotwal inquired. There was silence. He shouted out the question again. This time a shabbily dressed man stepped forward. "Sahib, I was coming to the market with my load of vegetables when I stumbled on the feet of this man who was lying in a dark alley with his feet sticking out. At first I thought he was drunk and had passed out but when I tried to wake him up, I saw there was blood on his body. I tried to awaken him nevertheless. But he did not move a finger. He was dead. As soon as I realised that he was dead I started shouting for help". The vendor became silent again as if his role in the play was over. "Did anyone move the body?", the Kotwal asked, yawning. "No Sahib", a chorus answered. He asked his assistants to inquire among the people about any relevant information and then come and join him as he went on to inspect the body.

He then proceeded to examine the body at close quarters. The body was still a little warm and stiffness had not yet set in. The victim had been slit on the throat skilfully. The wound appeared fresh. Their was no other visible mark of assault on the body but that would be known completely only after post mortem. He ordered his assistants to collect all possible artefacts they could find near the body. The victim appeared to be in his late thirties or early forties. He was a muslim as suggested by his tunic which was tied to the right. His beard had few tinges of grey. The Kotwal ordered the body to be shifted to the Kotwali before shifting it to the Royal morgue. Maybe someone who recognised the man would come looking for him. He left one assistant behind at the scene and rode back to his Kotwali to have a hearty breakfast. As soon as the sound of the Kotwal's horse died down, people herded together again for a fresh round of gossip regarding the murder.

✪✪✪✪✪✪

Five

MURDER IN THE MARKET PLACE

Radha walked back home in a daze. The noises in her mind refused to die down. Finding the stranger again in the marketplace had been a shock and then the sudden news of the murdered man. She found it impossible to distract her thoughts from the stranger and the curious incidents since last night. Such thoughts were racing through her mind as she walked and before she could realize, she had reached home. Radha tried to compose herself as she entered the Haveli. Her mother, she always thought, had the sharpest ears imaginable and could hear her softest footstep. She had just crossed the main door that her mother asked for the sandalwood.

"The shopkeeper had not arrived yet Amma, I will get it for you later in the day."

"No need for you to go out again, I will send Mukundi after some time", her mother replied.

Radha climbed up the steps to her room.

"Your father will be returning today Radha", her mother shouted. "A messenger from the court had come to tell."

"Yes Amma", Radha replied.

Radha's father had been away for about a week with a few more officers. They had been assessing the produce of lands in the villages neighboring Agra and Mathura.

Her father was a busy man these days as the taxation of farmers was being revised. Raja Todar Mal was an astute statistician and wanted perfection from his officers. She was expecting him in the afternoon but it was late in the evening when her father reached home. Radha's mother had been waiting impatiently for him since morning.

"What took you so long? I was expecting you by late morning. Was the journey comfortable?" she asked.

Bihari Mal was a tall, healthy man of about forty five. While Mukundi helped him wash his hands and feet, Radha came and greeted him. Bihari Mal's face lit up on seeing his daughter.

"The journey was not so bad, but I was called to the fort as soon as I entered Agra by Todar Mal Sahib. One of an important officers of the court was found murdered today in the bazaar. Everyone was being questioned about him."

Radha tried to look indifferent and hoped she succeeded.

"Who was murdered father?", she asked casually.

"Not anyone from our office. He turned out to be an officer by the name of Hasan", replied her father.

She did not want to show any interest in what her father was telling though she strained her ears not to miss out a single word. So the murdered man belonged to the Royal court, she thought.Could the stranger be involved in it? Should she tell her father about last night? Maybe the stranger had no connection with this incident at all and she was just imagining things that were not.

She decided not to tell her father about last night and was surprised at her decision. She consulted her father always in matters that were important to her. She trusted his wisdom and experience more than anyone. She started feeling guilty of keeping the stranger's secret and yet she could not tell it to anyone. Her father had started to eat and asked about her painting. They talked about his stay in the villages. While her parents still talked quietly, she skipped away to her room.

Meanwhile, by afternoon, Hasan's body had been shifted from the Kotwali to the Royal morgue as no one had come to claim it. The tiny insignia of the court on his tunic, had led them to believe that he must have worked for the Emperor. The arrival of the body in the Royal morgue had been immediately followed by it's discovery. Hasan Ali had quarters within the fort and lived alone.

The Kotwal was immediately sent for and on his arrival, Assad Khan, the Chief Royal spy, went into a conference with him. The Kotwal, now a happier man after two full meals of breakfast and lunch, apprised Assad Khan about the discovery of the body.

"Not many clues could be gained from the scene of the murder", the Kotwal said. Assad Khan was in deep thought. Although he was a gentle looking man, he had a sharp brain and a very logical mind. The Kotwal, used to throwing his weight around people was perfectly well behaved in his presence.

"Last evening, as is the ritual, Hasan Ali came to report to me about the day's work. There was nothing out of the ordinary in his behavior", Assad Khan said softly.

"Sir, which province was he a spy for?"asked the Kotwal.

"Not a Mughal province, he was working as a spy for Mewar. He had just returned a few days back."

Assad Khan fell quiet again. Kotwal did not want to disturb his chain of thought. After some time Assad Khan spoke up, "Kotwal, I want you to go to the bazaar tomorrow at the same time that Hasan was murdered. Start questioning the vendors who are regular at that time for anything unusual they might have noticed this morning. Find out if anyone had seen him talking to somebody. Interview everyone thoroughly. I do not want any detail linked to the murder to be missed."

"Yes Sir, although my subordinates have questioned people today, we will question them again tomorrow!" the Kotwal replied and took leave.

Assad Khan had never felt such uneasiness before. Hasan was one of his best spies. His untimely death had come both as a shock and a personal loss. It was strange that such a brilliant spy who had come back from Mewar without any accident should be murdered in broad daylight in his own city. He somehow had a strong intuition that his death was in some way connected to his Mewar mission.

Assad Khan then called for Haider Khan. Haider was Hasan's best friend in the fort.They used to spend as much time together as was possible. Haider had been recruited in the spy service a couple of years back. Originally from Kabul, his quiet nature and good spying skills had made him a favorite with the Chief. In fact it was Hasan who had introduced him to Assad Khan. A visibly disturbed Haider was more sombre than his usual self. He was mourning for his dead friend.

✪✪✪✪✪✪

Six

A SLEEPLESS NIGHT

Radha lay wide awake in her bed. The cool night breeze was a blessing after the hot and busy day. She thought of the man lying dead in the street. She thought of the stranger walking past her in the bazaar. She turned to her side and then turned again. Sleep still eluded her. Finally she sighed and got up.

She was about to get out from her bed when someone lurched into the room from the window. Had she been expecting the stranger? Was that the reason she could not fall asleep? It was him.

"Welcome back", was what she felt like saying, but she kept quiet. Suraj was slightly taken aback at her lack of surprise. He had expected to find her asleep.

"What's your name?", he blurted out when he wanted to say so many things to her.

Radha was angry by now. "You can ask me my name and enter my room at night but I have no right to know your name or what you're doing here."

"Firstly I'm a stranger in this city and secondly I'm being chased. Somehow your room appears a perfect hiding place for the night. Can I ask you for a favor?" asked Suraj.

"That depends entirely on the favor", Radha smiled back and the tension between them immediately disappeared.

"Can I get something to eat. Unless I eat something I will not have the strength to climb down your window", Suraj gathered the courage to say.

Radha was in a dilemma. She knew it would be difficult to manage food for him from the kitchen below. Yet she wanted him to eat something. She softly slipped out of the room with the lantern in her hand and bolted it from outside. She was wary of the stranger and did not want him roaming in the Haveli. She tiptoed into the kitchen and looked about for food. Mukundi coughed. Radha stood petrified for some time, frightened that either her parents or Mukundi would wake up.

Finally, when all was quiet again, she came back to her room with whatever was left of the dinner. Suraj ate hungrily. He had had a tough day running and hiding.

He needed a safe place at night. He did not want to be murdered in the streets of Agra while he slept unawares. Radha watched him eat. When he finished eating, she spoke up. "I cannot let you sleep in my room. Last night was a different story. I was not aware of your presence, but not tonight. My father is here. He is an officer in the Royal court. He will be out of his mind if he comes to know about your presence in his house."

Suraj was already feeling better. He had not talked to a single person the whole day and he felt like confiding in Radha. He did not know the reason, perhaps it was the strain of the past few days or the lack of conversation. He decided to tell her his story, if not fully,in parts.

"Would you let me stay till daybreak. It must be past midnight already", asked Suraj hesitantly yet hopefully.

"I cannot let you spend the night here. I know nothing about you", Radha retorted.

"Nor do I know anything about you," laughed Suraj.

Radha stared back at him and he took a deep breath. He would have to tell her about himself if he wanted to spend the night here.

"My name is Surya Pratap Singh. I come from Chittor, the capital of Mewar. I train horses and had come to apply for the same post at a friend's recommendation in the Mughal army."

"The stranger has a name now, Surya Pratap", thought Radha.

"Why are you running and from whom? What have you done?", she asked aloud.

"It is something I cannot share with you at present. It involves names of many nobles and you can appreciate the privacy that royalty demands. Trust me, I have done nothing wrong", replied Suraj.

There was a sincerity in his voice and something more. An appeal to let him stay for the night, an appeal to trust him.

"Are you aware that a murder took place in the market place today morning?" Radha looked at him searchingly.

"No, I'm not!" Suraj sat bolt upright, as if awakened from a dream.

"That's a little difficult to believe", Radha said accusingly. "It occurred around the same time that I saw you in the market place."

"That does not mean that I saw or heard about it. It must have happened after I left the bazaar", Suraj defended himself but his mind was racing elsewhere.

Radha was not convinced. She had a strong intuition about his connection with the murder and more so as he was always looking for a place to hide.

"If you choose to be mysterious, you may, but I think it is not fair that I give you shelter and food and get dishonesty in return."

Suraj saw that there was no point explaining.

"Do you know who was killed?"

Radha described what she had heard in the market place and from her father about the victim.

Suraj had never imagined that he was in for such a rude shock. He became pensive and silent. Hasan's murder was the last thing he wanted to hear today.

"Trust me, I won't bother you for long. Just a few days more in Agra and my job is done. It's best for you to know as little as possible about me."

Radha did not probe him further. She had heard so much about the Chittorgarh fort. She wanted to paint it someday. "I have always wanted to see the fort of Chittor. Is it bigger than the fort at Agra?", she asked.

"Much bigger and older and majestic." replied Suraj with pride.He talked about the fort of Chittorgarh. It was situated on a hill of the Aravalli range, sprawled over a huge area and was a city in itself, he explained. The remaining hours flew away describing the beauty of the fort, the life inside it and the sieges it had suffered and recovered from.

At the magical moment of pre dawn when the darkness of the night surrenders finally to the light, Suraj thanked Radha and bade her farewell. He slipped away in the last fading hours of the darkness of the night. When he was turning the street he suddenly realized that he had again forgotten to ask her name. He felt a strange longing to go back and ask her. Maybe he would never see her again. The thought itself made him anxious. He continued to walk, pushing away the desire to go back to her. Hasan's murder had complicated his situation further.

Radha, continued to look out of the window for long. She was no longer angry with him.

✪✪✪✪✪✪

Seven

THE EMPEROR'S HUNT

The Emperor's hunting prowess was a natural gift. His aversion to reading and writing since childhood was partly due to his constant urge to spend time with animals. Right from his teen years, when he had fiercely battled a tigress while returning from Malwa, he had grown fearless with each hunt. At times such as now, when he was not directly involved in battle, he always went for a hunt to exercise. It was also a way of intimidating the enemy and keeping the army prepared.

The preparations for the "Qumargah" were under way. The Emperor was getting impatient as a delay of a few days had been announced by Man Singh. He always hunted atop his favorite elephant Hawai. Hawai would lead him safely to the centre of the forest where all the animals would have been herded over days by the drummers. Man Singh had informed him that Hawai was showing symptoms of indigestion. Although his diet was always monitored, yet nothing in the fort premises could ever be beyond suspicion. With so many attempts on the Emperor's life already, it would not be surprising if someone tried to tamper with Hawai's food and drink before the hunt. The Emperor would never leave without Hawai and considering the present circumstances, a delay in the hunt was inevitable. The Emperor felt restless. He could not march into battle every time there was a minor rebellion, now that he was Emperor. Hunting was the best way to occupy his time and keep the army active.

The Mughal style of hunting, which involved the use of the army as beaters to make a "Qumargah" or enclosure was favored by his ancestors, Chengiz Khan and Timur. The soldiers acted as beaters, forming a huge circle and driving the game towards the centre. This time it was planned to surround an area of about sixty miles diameter by fifty thousand beaters over a time of one month. The Emperor would then ride to the centre of the circle, about four miles wide where all the animals would be gathered and he alone would hunt along with his closest nobles. He was fond of hunting using different kinds of weapons; a bow and arrow, a sword, a lance, a musket or even a lasso. He loved hunting for days, after which the nobles were allowed to take their turn and after them the servants of the court and finally the troopers. It was not uncommon for people to make use of the confusion that prevailed towards the end of the hunt sometimes to settle private scores.

The activity in the Royal household and Harem was also at its peak as a few Queens were expert in hunting. It was still undecided who would accompany the Emperor this time. The Persian Queen, Begum Rukkaiya, was his personal favorite for the hunts but the Emperor was known for springing a surprise at the last moment. The Hindu Queen, Hira Kunwari, the princess of Amber before marriage, was also a strong contender this time. Her nephew Man Singh would be the Emperor's close companion during the hunt.

Meanwhile, the Emperor was still oblivious of the murder of Hasan as Assad Khan did not consider it significant enough to disturb him before the hunt. He was hopeful that he would be able to bring the culprit to book before the Emperor's return. He was aware of the young Jalalluddin's passion for hunting and had accompanied him once. His fearlessness with wild animals had left him awed. Though he would not be accompanying him this time, some of his subordinates would.

Assad Khan had officially begun investigating the murder of Hasan Ali. An orphan, who had been recruited in the army by his relatives, Hasan had no immediate family. The fort was his home and his closest friend was Haider.

He decided to interrogate Haider Khan first. He wanted a detailed account of Hasan's activities in the last few days. When Haider arrived in his quarters he was still gloomy. He said that he had noticed nothing unusual.

"Hasan was his normal cheerful self. He did not appear to have anything on his mind", said Haider.

"Did you notice any change in his routine?", asked Assad Khan.

"No Sir", Haider replied.

"Where were you yesterday morning?"

"In my rooms in the fort Sir. I had just finished my lunch, when I was informed of the incident."

"Who informed you?"

"The guard posted in our quarters Sir. The news of Hasan's death had spread fast after the arrival of his body", replied Haider.

"Haider, I know you are mourning your friend's death deeply, but I would like you to bear with me and answer a few more questions", Assad Khan said to Haider.

"There is nothing more I want right now than the culprit being caught. I would do anything to help you Sir. I am shaken and intrigued with this sudden tragedy", Haider replied with passion.

"Did Hasan have any other close friends besides you?", asked Assad Khan.

Haider hesitated. "Not close friends I would say, but just a couple of days back a horse trainer had arrived from Chittor whom Hasan had befriended while he was on duty in Chittor. It was on Hasan's recommendation that he was recruited in the cavalry."

"Chittor...." murmured Assad Khan. He had sent Hasan there a few months back, in the winter season, to review the Rana's army. He was not aware that he had made a friend there.

"Anyone else besides him?", asked Assad Khan

Haider hesitated, opened his mouth and was silent again. Assad Khan waited for him to speak.

He replied in the negative. "Hasan had no other real friends."

"Haider, I know you would not like to discuss Haider's private life, especially now that he is gone. But it's imperative for us to find the murderer. He was a very dependable and intelligent spy. He was not one to be murdered for nothing. His murder definitely has ramifications on the security of the fort and the Emperor. Anything connected with Hasan is a clue for us. You know this better than anybody." Assad Khan paused and waited for Haider to reply.

"Sir, Hasan was a dear and only close friend of mine. We had no secrets between us. There was a girl he used to visit regularly for the past one year. He met her secretly because she's married. They met often, as often as work allowed him, but I don't think he ever discussed his work with her."

Assad Khan's interest was aroused. "This is an important lead Haider. If Hasan was indeed close to this lady as you say, we will have to interview her. Who is she? Where does she live?"

Haider informed him about the lady requesting Assad Khan to be discreet about the enquiry.

"Don't worry about it. The first duty of a spy is secrecy. And that's what we all are first."

Haider Khan left.

✪✪✪✪✪✪

Eight

THE SECRET

Suraj had been shocked on hearing about the victim's identity. The plot was getting thicker. He was clueless and friendless. His supply of money was fast dwindling. The danger of being recognized and captured was lurking like an evil shadow.

Ever since he had come to know of the secret he had been on the run. He had decided to share his knowledge with Hasan and had left a message with him to meet in the market place, and now Hasan was no more. He was murdered in cold blood early in the morning. Suraj himself had been in the vicinity at that time. His life was in equal danger and he had an intuition that his absence from the fort would be mistaken for guilt. It was urgent to reach the palace and meet the concerned authorities, but he also knew that as soon as he entered the fort he would be captured. Still, he could not keep the knowledge to himself. How he wished he had Pratap by his side to ask for advice.

He thought of the girl with the dark eyes. She had mentioned that her father was an officer in the court. It was her father who had first told her of Hasan Ali's real identity. He had forgotten to ask her name, yet again. Was he thinking of seeking her help as an excuse to meet her again, he wondered. It was a beautiful excuse nonetheless, he thought, and cheered up for a while. Perhaps it was providence that he had taken refuge in her room and her father had easy access to the fort.

Could he enter the court with her father's help? He recollected that last night she had been in dread of his visit being revealed to her father. It would be unrealistic to ask her father for help. She was the only person he knew in Agra besides Hasan Ali and the contact mentioned by Pratap. He was in a dilemma whom to turn to. Going back to Chittor was the easiest and most pragmatic option. But not for a Suryavanshi Rajput. For them truth was foremost, even at the cost of life. Running away to Chittor without conveying the knowledge he had acquired would not only be cowardly but lower him in his own eyes and those of Pratap's. Pratap was the epitome of Rajputana pride and valor.

He had to find a way of entering the court without being caught.

While Suraj debated with himself on the streets of Agra, Radha went to the market place again. In the excitement following her father's return, her mother had forgotten to send Mukundi to buy sandal wood. Radha found an easy excuse for leaving the house. The real reason was that she found it difficult to remain inside the house. She had managed only a few hours sleep but she hardly felt sleepy. Her restlessness got the better of her and she decided to go out. Her mother was happy now that her father was finally home and spent most of the day preparing food for him along with Lata. Radha told her mother she was going to buy sandalwood and quickly slipped out of the house, before her mother could call her back. She walked in the direction of the market with the secret hope of meeting Suraj again in the marketplace.

It was another day at the market, no different from the previous ones. People were busy with their daily chores and the murder of one Hasan Ali was already a distant memory.

Not so for the Kotwal. He had to prepare a report for Assad Khan by afternoon. Getting up early in the morning to reach the market place had been an unpleasant but unavoidable task. He divided the shops among his two assistants and asked them to make inquiries about the previous morning. He decided to interview the vegetable and fruit vendors himself. Their stock, fresh from the farms, appeared more lucrative. His inquiries and those of his assistants, drew a blank. No one had seen Hasan prior to his death. There had been no remarkable incident before the murder last morning.

While the Kotwal and his assistants were busy with their investigation, Suraj was conducting his own little private one. He retraced his steps along the alley he had taken yesterday, observing for any tell-tale signs of the murder though he had little hope of finding anything. He felt the constant threat of being recognised by someone from the fort and so decided to change his appearance a little. He decided to buy himself a new pair of clothes. As he neared the shops he noticed the Kotwal mounted on his horse. He decided to try another market for food and clothes. He had taken a few steps forward when he saw Radha coming towards him. Both stopped midway. It was while standing in the middle of the street, seeing the girl again that Suraj had an epiphany. The solution to his problem flitted across his mind like a dream. He passed Radha and whispered to her to follow him. She followed him at a distance and when they reached a safe distance from the market Suraj waited for her to catch up. "Can you take me to a place where we can talk without being noticed?", he asked Radha.

"Yes", said Radha, simply. She knew where to take him. It was a very old Neem tree on the banks of the Yamuna, near the southern wall of the fort. There had been a couple of drowning deaths at this spot last year and people avoided it considering it an ill-fated site. Radha took the lead and in about half an hour, she and Suraj were sitting in the shade of the old tree.

✪✪✪✪✪✪

Nine

BY THE BANKS OF THE YAMUNA

The tree was old, with arms spread out wide, giving a cool shade to those who took it's shelter. It had witnessed many a lovers' whispers, sweet nothings and tiffs, the sound sleep of weary travelers and children chasing each other. It had witnessed the rise and fall of the Yamuna waters. It has witnessed the drownings of weary souls, tired of the burden called life. It had borne the excesses of the sun and rain with equal love. It never gave in to fury like the waters of the Yamuna, sister of Yama, for it was an extension of the earth, giving without asking in return.

The wall of a Agra the fort was visible from the banks. The Emperor, who was rumored to stay awake till very late into the night, sometimes enjoyed boat trips on the

Yamuna, on full moon nights, when the waters sparkled like silver. Right now, the waters glistened like diamonds, reflecting the sunlight like a mirror. There was not a soul in sight.

Under the cool and comfortable shade of the Neem tree, sat Radha and Suraj. Both felt reassured by the loneliness of the spot. Suraj was thirsty. It was still well before noon, but the heat of the sun was bearing down on the city of Agra. Radha sensed his discomfort.

"Why didn't you tell me before", she said.

"What?" asked a puzzled Suraj.

"That you are thirsty", replied Radha.

"But I never said that now", replied an even more perplexed Suraj. Was he mumbling his thoughts aloud without even realizing, he thought.

"It's quite obvious. You look thirsty and exhausted. There is a drinking well not far from here. Let's go there", Radha looked at him in concern. It looked like he had been bereft of food and drink since the night before.

"Later, you can take me there on the way back. Right now I have an urgent favor to ask of you."

Radha looked at Suraj and realized at that very moment, that she would help him, even if it meant going out of her way to do so.

"Depends on what you want from me", she lied.

"You know I'm a wanted man. I am a fugitive from

the court. But I am a fugitive with a secret. A secret which concerns the Emperor himself. A secret which I am under no obligation to disclose to anyone. But what I know must be revealed, and only to the person it concerns", said Suraj

"The Emperor!"exclaimed Radha.

"Yes, and I am also the prime suspect in the murder that took place yesterday."

"I thought so", Radha said softly, more to herself.

"You don't think that I am involved in the murder in anyway, do you?", asked Suraj.

Radha did not reply. Her silence was unsettling for Suraj.

"Do you think I'll kill my own friend?", asked Suraj with some anger.

"Your friend?", Radha blurted out, unable to hide her surprise.

"Yes, if the murdered man was Hasan, a spy in the Royal secret service".

"That's what my father told me", Radha said drawing patterns on the ground with a twig.

The waters of the Yamuna were glittering in the sunlight. The spot being desolate, no one was in sight. There were a few dark clouds, harbingers of the pre-monsoon showers, playing hide and seek with the sun. The summer heat had become too much to bear and a few good showers would be welcome before the monsoons finally made the Yamuna waters dance to their tunes. Soon the sun hid behind a flitting cloud. The sudden coolness was relieving. Radha continued playing with the twig.

Suraj looked at her for sometime. "It might be difficult for you to believe, but I am in no way involved in Hasan's death. I will tell you why, but later. Meanwhile my message needs to be conveyed to the Emperor. If I enter the fort it would mean imminent arrest. Your father enters the fort daily. Can he pass on the message to Todar Mal?"

Radha looked up sharply.

"No, I cannot discuss our meeting with father", she said vehemently. Suraj knew he could not press her on this issue and he kept quiet.

"But I can help pass on your message. What is it you want to convey?", she inquired after a while, feeling bad that she had snubbed him when he had asked for help.

Suraj was already beaming. "What I'm about to tell you should remain with you only till you pass it on to the Emperor." Radha nodded her head and listened to Suraj's tale without interrupting.

By the time he had finished a slight breeze had started. The shade of the tree and the breeze had a soothing effect on Suraj. He felt like sleeping. Last night had again been a sleepless one. Radha and Suraj sat in silence, each busy with their own thoughts. Radha was thinking about conveying Suraj's message to the court without involving her father. Suraj was looking at Radha lost deep in thought, unaware of his gaze on her. A cuckoo started to coo somewhere in the branches of the tree. Her persistent soulful sound brought them back to their surroundings. Suraj wanted to take a nap. Radha got up dusting her skirt. "I think it's time I returned home. Amma will be getting worried. She might even send Mukundi to look for me."

"I think it's a nice place to catch up with some sleep", said Suraj.

"Are you not thirsty?", asked Radha.

"Tell me the way to the well. I'll go there when I get up. Right now all I want to do is lie down and close my eyes", he replied.

Radha gave him directions to the well and bade goodbye. Just as she was about to leave, she remembered that she had a few silver coins left with her. "Take these. You'll need them to buy food and new clothes" , she said.

"I still have some money left with me. It will last me a couple of days. I do not plan to stay here for long anyways. If I need money I'll definitely ask you for help", Suraj replied with a twinkle in his eyes.

Radha got miffed. "As you wish", she said and turned back.

"I'll meet you tonight", Suraj replied to her retreating back, chuckling to himself. Somehow it felt nice that he could make her angry.

He lay back on the soft grass and soon fell asleep. He woke up with a start. There was a sound growing louder and nearer, the sound of heavy feet stealthily advancing towards the tree. Suraj got up and started to run. The man behind him started to run too. Suraj dared not look back and continued to run. And then he saw her sitting by the river, her long hair flowing to the waist. He wanted to call out to her for help, but he realized that he did not know her name. His throat turned dry and he panicked. The cuckoo was cooing but even she did not know her name.

He woke up and it took him some time to realize he had been dreaming. He sighed with relief. He had forgotten to ask her name. What was wrong with him? He was not the Suraj he used to be. Tonight the first thing he would do on meeting her would be to ask her name. His throat was parched. He draped the turban cloth he had been using as a pillow around his head and started out in search of the well.

✪✪✪✪✪✪

Ten

A DISCREET MEETING

Meanwhile Assad Khan was busy with his investigation. The Kotwal's visit to the site of the murder had not yielded much information. His sixth sense which was his strength as a spy was telling him that Hasan Ali's death had other implications. He had not died without a reason. Unfortunately he had not a single piece of evidence to start with. There was no suspect he could lay his finger on and so he decided to meet the lady Haider had told him about. Perhaps she would be the best person to apprise him about Hasan's thoughts and activities the day before he met his untimely death. He would have to be discreet about this meeting as the lady in question was married to a respectable man. This had been the reason for Haider's reluctance in disclosing her name. He had found out that the lady's husband was a senior artist in the Tasvir Khana. He decided to visit the begum in the afternoon when her husband would be away at the Tasvir Khana where the Royal artists were always busy painting the Emperor's conquests and adventures.

Her house was not in the fort premises. It was close to the Tasvir Khana where quarters had been especially built for the artists. They had easy access to the bazar where their unending demand of colors and paints was easily met with. Was it possible that Hasan was leaving from the Begum's house that morning after spending the night there, thought Assad Khan as he entered the artists' colony. He asked a group of children who were flying kites for Mir Mohammad's house. One young lad, tired of holding the roll of string while his friend soared the kite, dropped the roll with glee and ran off to show him the house. His friend shouted and cursed him from behind, swearing never to fly kites with him again.

Assad Khan thanked the little boy on reaching the house and knocked at the door. He had to wait for some time before an elderly housemaid came to open the door. Assad Khan told her to inform the begum that an officer from the court had come to meet her. She came back with the message that Mir Saheb was at the Tasvir Khana and he could go and meet him there. He sent her back with the message that it was the lady of the house he wanted to meet about something urgent. This time he was allowed to enter and made to wait in the main hall. The maid came back with a glass of khus sherbet and then left. Assad Khan sat sipping the sherbet, waiting for the Begum to appear. The house was modestly and sparsely decorated. There were no sounds of any children. Perhaps they were playing outside.

Assad Khan got up as soon as Mehrunissa Begum entered the waiting room. She was wearing a nakab and he could only see her eyes. They were large, black and beautiful but appeared red and swollen from crying. She was short, slightly plump and he placed her to be in her early thirties. After greeting Assad Khan she sat down opposite him and waited. Assad Khan sensed that she was not in a mood to broach the conversation. He was weighing his words. He would have to be careful of what he said. "I want to assure you that whatever conversation takes place now will never go beyond me."

She looked up at him with a jerk, surprise in her eyes. "Who are you?" she asked.

"I am Assad Khan, Chief of the Royal Spy Service. I am investigating the murder of Hasan Ali. I have reason to believe you knew him", he said.

Her eyes withdrew immediately. She lowered her head, perhaps fighting with her emotions. She did not answer him.

"I hope you are aware that he was murdered yesterday morning, slit on the neck." She nodded in acquiescence. Assad Khan continued. "I have no lead whatsoever to start my investigation. But you would agree that the culprit should be brought to justice. He cannot be allowed to roam free."

Mehrunissa was visibly going through a dilemma. She swallowed, tried to speak but failed to. Assad Khan waited patiently. Finally she spoke up.

"Hasan was a good friend. To call him a very good friend would not be a lie. He was perfectly his normal gentle self the day before.I had met him in the evening."

"Did he meet you daily?" asked Assad Khan.

"Whenever possible yes", she replied.

"Did he mention anything unusual to you of late? Something he was nervous or excited about?"

Mehrunissa thought for a while. "He was very happy when he came back from Chittor. He said he made a very good friend and that he was an excellent horse trainer. He was in awe of his expertise with horses and how someone could understand them so well. He was very fond of horses himself. He had suggested him to join the Mughal army. He had become really fond of his new friend and often spoke of him."

"Did he tell you why he went to Chittor?" asked Assad Khan.

"No, he never discussed his work. It was only about this person that he had discussed with me and so I found it unusual. Perhaps he was deeply impressed with him", Mehrunissa replied.

Assad Khan had never doubted Hasan's skills as a spy and knew he never discussed work with anyone.

"Did he mention anything else about his trip to Chittor?" he inquired.

"No, not about Chittor, but last week he told me that the friend he had met in Chittor had come to Agra at his suggestion and he was hopeful he would be able to get him a place in the cavalry," she replied.

"Did he ever happen to mention his name?" asked Assad Khan.

"No, never. He was a Rajput. That is all I know about him", she replied.

A Rajput from Mewar, being recruited by Hasan, a Mughal spy. A spy who had been deputed to spy on the army of Rana Udai Singh. Something was out of place, thought Assad Khan. Why had Hasan never discussed about this horse trainer with him. Assad Khan asked for permission to leave.

"I hope that next time I meet you it will be with news about who was behind this cowardly act. Please be assured that whatever has been discussed is for my ears only." Assad Khan departed with some lead to work on. Both Haider Khan and Mehrunissa had highlighted the growing closeness between the Rajput and Hasan.This was a lead which was most important and lay at the core of the matter.

✪✪✪✪✪✪

Eleven

RADHA'S DILEMMA

Radha hurried back home. The sun was out from behind the clouds. She had lost track of time while talking to Suraj. She was hoping that her father would have left for the court without waiting for her to come back. When she reached home she tried to sneak up to her room, but her mother had sharp eyes and sharper ears. "What took you so long in the market place ?" she asked coming out into the courtyard on hearing Radha's footsteps. Radha kept climbing the steps.

"The shop selling sandalwood was still shut when I reached the marketplace and the shopkeeper I buy colors from had finished his stock of red. So I had to wait till his boy got it from the godown", she replied without looking back.

She was amazed at herself for lying to her mother. She rarely lied to her mother. She sat down in her room and filled a glass of water from the pitcher. Suraj should find the well easily. She wanted to help him, but could not justify herself. Was it the break in the monotony and the thrill involved? She sighed. Somethings are better left unexplained she thought. Maybe she just believed in his story and wanted to convey his message across. Telling father about him would be full of risks and would end in a failure.

"Radha, do you want to have lunch right now or later?" shouted Lata from below.

Lata's life is so simple thought Radha. All she thinks is of feeding us and her family while her husband thinks of feeding the Royal household. And suddenly, she knew how she could help Suraj. She had thought of a plausible way to convey Suraj's message. Lata's husband Magan, was a cook in the palace. She knew him well and he was a simple person. Could she not request him to pass on Suraj's message to a reliable person in the court? There was some hope in sight. Something she could think about.

"Lata I am coming down. Let us have our lunch", she shouted back.

After awhile she skipped down the flight of stairs and sat on the kitchen floor besides her mother.

"It has become so hot and there is still no sight of rains. The rain Gods are not happy", her mother complained. Her mother had a God to complain for every occasion and also to be grateful for. Radha ate in silence, preoccupied with her thoughts. She waited for her mother to leave for her afternoon nap. She wanted to talk to Lata alone. After lunch Radha kept herself busy with Lata in the kitchen. Soon she heard her mother's soft and steady snoring.

"Lata, does your husband go to the Emperor's kitchen daily?", she asked casually.

"Yes, he gets a weekly off on Fridays", Lata replied.

"I have always been very curious about how they cook for the Emperor. I've heard so many stories about how many times people have tried to poison his food. Is it true ?" she asked her.

"I have no idea about the stories but the supervision in the kitchen is very strict. That is what Magan always tells me. Each food item is fed to a cat and sometimes even servants before sending it to the Emperor", Lata replied.

"Oh! It sounds so fascinating. Can I accompany him some day. Father has never taken me to the palace with him. Would you request him to take me along?",Radha pleaded.

"What would you do in the kitchen Radha? As it is,I don't think they let strangers enter the Royal kitchen. The Emperor and his Queens are very particular about what they eat and drink."

"I have also heard that the kitchen walls have paintings of the Emperor so that the cooks feel his presence. I wanted to have a look at them closely. Can't he take me along for just one day? I'm sure he knows enough people there to let me accompany him", Radha pleaded.

"If you are so keen, I'll ask him. But just because you're insisting. I can't promise anything right now", said Lata. "I'm going to take a nap now", she added and left the kitchen.

Radha went back to her room and resumed her painting. Soon the stillness of the afternoon lulled her senses and she put her weary head on the pillow. She had no idea of time and it was well past sunset when she woke up. She realized how tiring the night and day had been when she had to make real efforts to get out of bed. Her father was back home and she wanted to show him her work which he had missed in his absence from home. The evening was spent over Radha's paintings and soon it was dinner time.

Radha rushed back to her room after dinner.

"This girl is always in a hurry these days. God only knows where her mind is," her mother complained to her father. Radha was hurrying up the steps to her room.

"She is just busy with her paintings. You know how passionate she is about them", her father replied. He was very proud of his daughter's talent with the brush. Radhe bolted her room from the inside. Having slept most of the day, she could not go to sleep.

She picked up her palate and started to mix the colors, then decided that the candle light was inadequate and so she'd complete it in sunlight. Finally she had nothing to do except follow her restless train of thoughts. When would Suraj be meeting her next? Had he found a safe place to rest for the night? Radha had always been proud of her indifference to boys of her age but this time her emotions for Suraj had surprised her. Though she was surprised she was not ashamed. If she liked meeting him, it had to be right. She loosened her hair and decided to put off the lamp, when there was a noise. She looked down the window into Suraj's smiling face. She looked around, suddenly frightened that someone might see him. The street was dark and deserted. She gave a hand to Suraj and he jumped into the room.

"Surprised?", he laughed.

"Not any longer. I would have been surprised had you not turned up", replied Radha. Suraj chuckled. "I had nowhere else to go in this city" he said.

"Why don't you go back to Chittor?", she asked.

"You know I can't. I have some unfinished work", Suraj replied.

"Finish it off fast, how long will you keep hiding and running!" Radha said.

"For that I need your help. The only person I knew in Agra has been murdered. My disappearance from the fort is being equated to my guilt", he replied.

Till now Radha had been looking away from him. She now looked into his soft brown eyes. They were large and kind. Maybe they were the reason that she trusted him. She looked away.

"I have an idea, it might help you to enter the court and meet the Emperor", she said

"Tell me about it", he replied distractedly.

"Lata, who cooks for us, lives inside the fort. Her husband is a cook in the Royal kitchen. He has been there for about three years now. I have requested her to ask him if I can accompany him tomorrow or as soon as possible". said Radha.

"What use would that be?", Suraj asked curtly.

"I could pass on your message to someone close to the Emperor", Radha replied.

"Why not simply pass on the message via the cook." asked Suraj.

"Well, do you think it would be safe to give him the message? It's your wish. If you have no problem with it I can ask him to deliver the message, but you had given me the impression that you wanted to involve as few people as possible in this discreet affair", retorted Radha.

Suraj smiled. "What's your name, before I forget to ask again."

Radha was taken aback at this sudden change in the conversation. It was at that moment she realized his ignorance of her name. She started laughing. "I'm Radha, Welcome to my room", she said.

Suraj's smile lit up his face.

"I think it's not a bad idea if not a great one either. I can't enter the fort for the fear of being recognized and arrested. You try to go there on some pretext and pass on my message to someone reliable and close to the Emperor", he said.

"Does that mean you trust me more than the cook?", smiled Radha.

"Beggars can't be choosers", Suraj replied with twinkling eyes.

"Yes, you are at my mercy now", laughed Radha.

She was getting excited about her plan of action. Today she had brought some food with her, anticipating Suraj's arrival. She got up and placed it quietly before him. He thanked her and ate in silence while she watched. He then got up and lay on the floor. Soon he was fast asleep. Radha checked that the room was bolted from inside and lay her head on the pillow. She thought of the enormity of the situation if her parents come to know about Suraj sleeping in her room. The thought made her shiver and she pushed it out her mind. She lay thinking and was asleep not long after.

✪✪✪✪✪✪

Twelve

ASSAD KHAN INVESTIGATES

As soon as he reached his chambers, Assad Khan sent for Haider Khan. He then asked for the recruiter of the horse trainers, Hari Dass, who was an excellent horse trainer himself, to be sent to him. Haider Khan was not in the fort. Assad Khan left a message with his subordinate to meet him on his return. Assad Khan sat in deep contemplation. Perhaps the Rajput from Chittor was the missing link he had been trying to find.

The cavalry was the most important part of the Mughal army and the Emperor paid fine attention to it. The horses were mostly of Arabian breed and the Emperor took personal interest in their breeding and training. He had introduced the system of "Mansabdars", in which each military officer was responsible for recruiting and maintaining his quota of horses. The rank of the officer depended on the number of horses he provided. Horses were carefully branded to avoid cheating. To look after such a large cavalry, the Emperor himself employed trainers and personal care-takers of horses, especially those of the higher officers. Hari Dass looked after recruiting such horse trainers.

He arrived in Assad Khan's chamber as soon as he got the message. Assad Khan greeted him and came to the point.

"Did you recently employ a Rajput from Chittor at Hasan Ali's recommendation?"

"Yes Sir, just three days back. A young man called Chandan. He understands horses like no other. He can even talk to them. His riding skills were also so brilliant that I kept him without any hesitation. He was with me almost that whole day but has been absent from work for the past two days. Today morning I had his quarters in the fort checked but there was no news of him", he replied.

"Did you inquire about his credentials before employing him?", asked Assad Khan. "Sir, you are aware that Hasan Ali was his strongest credential and his exemplary prowess with horses was another. I asked him why he wanted to join the Mughal army and he replied for money. He said he needed money for his family", Hari Dass replied.

"Did you ask him about his family? Where they were living?" asked Assad Khan.

"He said his parents and younger sister lived in Ajmer. He had gone to Chittor to look for a job when he had met Hasan Ali. I have a feeling he has gone to inform his parents or bring them with him to Agra. He looked sincere and in need of the job", said Hari Dass.

"Is there any reason for this inquiry about him?", he continued after some time. "Chandan came across as an honest person, well-behaved and professional and I did not expect him to disappear without information".

"Yes, there is a definite reason. His sudden disappearance is a matter of concern.Hasan Ali was found dead yesterday morning in the main Agra bazaar, murdered. We are trying to trace his activities in the past few days."Assad Khan replied.

"I know about the death Sir. Personally I do not think Chandan's absence is linked to it in any way. They both were on the best of terms. I strongly feel he was compelled to leave due to some personal reason."

"That time will tell. Thank you for your help. Should Chandan come back, which seems highly unlikely, needless to say you'll inform me without delay", replied Assad Khan. Hari Dass nodded and left his chambers.

Haider Khan was not back in the court before late evening. He immediately left for Assad Khan's chambers on his return.

"I have been waiting for you since morning, where have you been?" asked Assad Khan on seeing him.

"Who can make a man busy at such a short notice except for his wife", Haider replied with a sigh. "We had gone to visit her brother who is not keeping well."

Assad Khan told him that the young Rajput whom Hasan had befriended, had not returned to his quarters in the fort since Hasan's murder.

"I am surprised to hear that. I thought they were good friends and he was employed at Hasan's recommendation. In fact I was expecting that he would come and meet me after hearing the news of Hasan's sudden death", said Haider Khan. Assad Khan was perplexed by the turn of events and needed to talk to the Rajput himself.

"You have had a long day. Thank you for coming to meet me immediately on your arrival. Go to your quarters and rest. We shall find out more about this Rajput tomorrow", he told Haider and both bade farewell for the night.

Assad Khan could not catch two winks that night.The mystery of the Rajput from Mewar deepened with every passing hour. Why did he disappear so suddenly. From the accounts of Mehrunissa Begum and Hari Dass, he seemed to be an affable and talented personality, admired by Hasan. Was he imagining things or was there indeed more than met the eye. From Begum Mehrunissa's account Chandan was close to Hasan. Then why did

Hasan not discuss much about him with Haider Khan? Especially when he had been recruited in the Royal cavalry. An important link was missing in the puzzle and Assad Khan would not rest till he found the missing link.

Early next morning he had ordered his boys to launch a massive hunt for the elusive Rajput. From Agra to Chittor, every street and corner was to be searched. He gave them three days time. The artist employed by the spy service to sketch likenesses was taken to Hari Dass. He described Suraj and the result was an amazing life like likeness. It was copied by other artists and distributed amongst the spies setting out to hunt for Suraj. The Kotwal was summoned and also handed over a copy and asked to be on the look out.The copy was to be shown to all the shop-keepers of the bazaar where the murder took place.

Assad Khan sent his most reliable spy to Chittor incognito. He was hopeful that he would be back with valuable information.

Assad Khan was edgy. He felt a strange connection between Hasan's murder and the Emperor, but could not lay his finger on the missing link. He did not want to broach the topic with thc Emperor till he had sufficient proof. Everyone in Agra was aware that the Emperor was preparing for his favorite pastime - the grand hunt and other activities were of little interest to him right now. The postponement of the hunt due to Hawai's illness had already made him impatient. Hopefully by the time the hunt was over he would have caught the culprit behind Hasan's death. He wanted the Emperor to enjoy his favorite sport peacefully.

His servant in waiting announced the arrival of Haider Khan. Assad Khan asked him to send him in. After proper greetings Haider Khan mentioned about the missing Rajput.

"Sir, after talking to you last I made some inquiries about the man Hasan had befriended. I tried to pick up conversations of Hasan that other spies had overheard." said Haider.

"And what did you find out?", asked Assad Khan.

"This friend of Hasan, called Chandan, was unduly inquisitive. He was overly interested in the fort architecture, even in the single day that he spent in the fort. Hasan was so bowled over by his horsing skills that he overlooked the fact that he could be a spy planted by Udai Singh", replied Haider.

Assad Khan continued pacing the room.

The sooner this man was caught the better.

"Sir, would you like me to go to Chittor?" asked Haider.

"No. I have sent one of my best men. You would be more helpful here. I would like you to go to Begum Mehrunissa's house and introduce yourself. Try and talk to her about Hasan's activities in the last few days in detail. Try to pick up some information about this Rajput

Chandan. Maybe she would speak more freely with you than she did with me." said Assad Khan.

"I will go there today afternoon", replied Haider. Saying this he left Assad khan's chambers.

Assad Khan then asked the Royal Hakim in charge of the morgue to be sent to him.

He had some doubts regarding the wound on Hasan's throat. It had been caused using a sharp object by a right handed man. The morgue surgeon had studied the wound in detail. Assad Khan waited for him patiently to ask a few questions.

✪✪✪✪✪✪

Thirteen

RADHA'S PLANS

Radha woke up early hoping to get Suraj something to eat before he left. She was in for a surprise. The room showed no signs of having had a visitor the night before. The window, like always was wide open. She instinctively ran to the window and looked about. The street was empty and still a little dark, laden with the suspense that dawn holds. She turned back and checked the room again, still unable to come to terms with the fact that Suraj had left. Perhaps she had missed seeing him as it was still dark. He had left without doubt and there was no trace of his presence. Radha felt the same anger creeping up, every time Suraj disappeared without informing her. It was also mixed with a dread that she would not see him again. She went back to bed and lay thinking about ways to enter the court. She had always been interested in the murals, frescoes, miniatures and other paintings of the court. The Emperor had employed the finest miniature artists to depict his adventures. She had once asked her father if he would take her along some day and he had promptly refused. He was very austere about his office and so she had never raised the subject again.

In the kitchen below she could hear Lata's arrival. Radha jumped out of bed and hurried with her daily ablutions. She wanted to meet Lata before her mother entered the kitchen. She hurried down to the kitchen. Lata raised her eyebrows in surprise on seeing her so early in the kitchen. She knew what was on Radha's mind.

"You are up very early today Radha", she said.

"I wanted to speak to you about the trip to the fort." Radha spoke up before Lata could question her further. "Did you talk to Magan about it?"

"Yes, I did." replied Lata, looking around to see that no-one was overhearing.

"What did he say?", asked Radha unable to hide her excitement."

"He says he will have to take the permission of the head cook who is very busy these days as there is a shortage of helpers. He will talk to him after a few days when the hiring of new helpers is complete."

Radha's face lit up. "That is very good news. If there is a shortage of helpers, can't Magan recommend me as a kitchen help ?" asked Radha.

Lata was surprised at Radha's urgency to go to the fort, even at the cost of being a kitchen help.

"Why this sudden hurry to go to the palace, Radha? If Amma comes to know she'll tell Baba and then all hell will break loose you know", warned Lata.

"Lata please do not discuss it with Amma or Baba", pleaded Radha. "I have to see the Queen's palace to complete my paintings. If I ask any of them for permission they will never let me set foot out of the house. This is the best time as any to go with Magan,so why postpone it?"

"That is why I do not want you to go, because your parents will be kept in the dark about it", said Lata as she kneaded the dough.

"Lata, it is the matter of a day only. I shall leave with Magan and come back with him. We shall tell Amma that I'm going to Gauri's house to help her with the wedding clothes", Radha said.

"Let me discuss it with Magan again. If he agrees to take you along as a helper for a day I have no problem. You are placing a big responsibility on my shoulders Radha," replied Lata reluctantly.

"Does not Magan go to the fort everyday in the morning and come back in the evening?" asked Radha.

"Yes, he does. But that is because he is doing a job there", said Lata.

"And all I'm asking is that I accompany him for one day. I shall help in the kitchen and whatever little free time I'll get I shall study the paintings in the unrestricted areas of the fort. Magan just has to take permission from the head cook if I can fill in for a helper for one or two days", Radha implored Lata.

Lata was silent. "I will talk to him", she replied after some time. Radha hugged her and left the kitchen. Her step was light as if a burden had been lifted off her mind. She was hopeful that Magan would agree to take her along. She thought of sharing her plans with Suraj but then decided against it. To meet him she would have to leave the house and look out for him, and she didn't want to raise her mother's suspicions. She decided to stay at home the whole day and busied herself with her paintings.

Meanwhile in the kitchen below Lata was faced with the mammoth dilemma of helping Radha with her plans or not. Magan would not refuse if she requested him because he adored Radha since he had known her as a child. She was like a daughter to him, that he never had, and always pampered her. She knew that if she told Amma, Radha's plans would be foiled forever. Amma would definitely tell Baba and that would be the end of Radha's dreams of visiting the fort. She had also realized that Radha was very keen and optimistic about her visit to the fort. Knowing Radha's headstrong nature, Lata was afraid that if she did not help her Radha might hatch another plan to visit the fort. Finally she decided that a day spent under Magan's care should be harmless.

✪✪✪✪✪✪

Fourteen

THE SARAI

He had to bide time again and was sure that by now there were orders to capture him. He was pining his hopes on Radha but that was not enough. She was still a young girl in-spite of having connections in the fort. He wondered if she was smart enough to get his message across to a reliable person. Would it not be more prudent of him to leave Agra in disguise and take refuge in Chittor or any other city of Mewar? No, he re-iterated to himself, he had to clear the air before leaving.

Now it was high time that he changed his appearance. Simply shaving off his beard would not serve any purpose. He needed a different set of clothes. He decided that later in the evening, he would to buy a Jama and turban that were popular in Agra, to mingle with the local crowd. He would have to wait till twilight to meet Radha and ask her how far she had proceeded with her plans. He strolled in the market and chose a barber shop that was busy so that no one would notice him. He then set out to eat. The entire day was before him. He had to live it in hiding.

Finally, after much deliberation and with nothing to do except hiding, he decided to meet the contact from Chittor whose address had been given to him by Pratap himself. Pratap had warned him not to approach the contact unless it was a dire emergency. Suraj knew that Pratap would himself justify the present situation as an emergency. He had to ask a few people for the directions to the Sarai whose address had been given to him by Pratap.

It was close to the outskirts of the city, for the convenience of travelers to get some food and a good night's rest. On entering the Sarai, he asked for the owner.

"He is in his room upstairs", replied a young boy serving some local wine to the customers.

"Can you go and tell him that the elephant seller has arrived", said Suraj. The young boy looked at him suspiciously. Suraj took his hand and placed a silver coin in it. The boy immediately put down his serving tray and ran up the stairs. He came down after a few minutes and beckoned Suraj to go up to the owner's room.

Suraj climbed the stairs wearily. He knocked at the door of the room. "Who is it?" a deep voice enquired.

"The elephant seller from Chittor", replied Suraj.

"Come on in", came the quick reply.

Suraj entered the room. The room was dark with little entry for the sun. Suraj greeted the owner who was sitting on the takht in a corner of the room. Two men were standing guard.

"You took a big risk by coming here", said the owner.

"I am aware of that. I was in a ticky situation. Finally I decided that it was better to spend the day here rather than out on the streets. I also needed a different set of clothes and could not risk buying them from the bazaar."

"What news do you bring?", asked the owner.

"It's a long story. Let me start from the beginning", replied Suraj.

"We have the whole day. I would rather prefer a long story", laughed the owner.

The owner was good company. Suraj felt relaxed and at ease with him. He ate a hearty meal after a long time. He changed into new clothes, tied a new turban and spent the evening sitting in the Sarai below. He looked a completely different person in his changed attire. No one noticed him though he noticed all who came and went. Late in the evening, there was music and dance and a boisterous atmosphere.

The hustle bustle of the wayfarers in the inn grew as the sun set. Suraj envied the fun and laughter of the travelers. He longed to be back in the streets of Chittor where he could roam freely and be with his friends. He decided it was not safe to venture out tonight though he was anxious to meet Radha. He was ready to return to his room when the owner sent a message that he wanted to meet him.

"I have just received some important information", he said.

"There is unprecedented scrutiny at the border. They are checking and frisking everyone entering or leaving Agra."

Suraj became pensive. The situation was more gloomy than he had presumed. Was it wise of him to get Radha, a total stranger involved? He hardly knew her and yet he had trusted her completely. Her father was working for the Emperor and his loyalties would always be to the Emperor. Tomorrow he would meet her and tell her to stay away from the matter. The lesser people came to know about his where abouts, the better it would be for him. He should not leave behind any footprints of his mission in Agra once he managed to leave the city for good. The owner was watching him. "Is anything the matter?", he asked Suraj.

"No, but tomorrow I shall leave the inn. It's not safe for me to stay at one place for long. This inn will soon be searched among other inns", said Suraj.

"You are right, as it is on the outskirts of Agra, it will be under observation always", replied the owner.

Soon, both Suraj and the owner retired to their rooms for the night.

✪✪✪✪✪✪

Fifteen

RADHA IN THE FORT

Radha's excitement and anxiety would not let her sleep. She glanced at the window frequently. She lay in bed thinking about Lata and Magan. Before Lata had left for the day, she had reminded her of talking to Magan. She was hoping that Lata would be able to convince her husband. Why was Suraj late tonight? Did she hear a footfall in the street? She ran to the window and looked both ways. There was no one in sight though it was too dark to make out anything clearly. She hoped he was safe and had not been apprehended by the Royal guards on the look out for him. Maybe he had found a safe place for the night. She knew he did not want to risk coming to her house again and again, though secretly she wished and prayed he would come quickly. Her prayers were unanswered that night. Waiting for him, she did not realize when she fell asleep.

She woke up as the morning light streamed into her room and the first thought that came to her mind was Suraj's absence. She decided not to give it much thought. Suraj was brave and intelligent enough to take good care of himself. Besides today was a day of activity for her.

She rushed down to meet Lata. She was a little early in her excitement. Lata had not yet arrived. Radha washed her face and drank some water and decided to wait for Lata in the kitchen. Lata came soon enough and laughed on seeing her. "This is the first time someone has welcomed me in the kitchen", she said.

"What news do you bring Lata? Can I accompany Magan today?", asked Radha impatiently. Lata smiled at Radha. "Yes, you can." Radha hugged Lata. "Thank you", was all she could say. "You can go with Magan as a help but only for one day. New cooks or assistants can only be recruited for one day at a time", added Lata.

"Oh, one day is enough for me. I cannot thank you and Magan enough", replied Radha.

"Get ready then. Magan leaves early. He might be coming any moment now. Last evening after talking to me he had gone to get a letter of permission for you from the head cook. You might as well go today and look at all the paintings to your heart's desire", said Lata.

Radha rushed to her room. She wore her best choli and skirt and carefully draped her dupatta. She went down to the kitchen again. Lata asked her to eat a little but she was too excited to eat anything. Suddenly, it dawned on her that her mother was not up yet.

"Lata, I have told Amma that I might be going to Gauri's house today. When she gets up please tell her that I left early so that I could be back early."

"I was wondering when you would think of Amma", said an amused Lata.

"How can you joke about it. Promise me that you'll convince her well", said Radha.

"Don't worry. You've already told her about your visit to Gauri's house. She will understand. Remember to be back home on time. That's more important."

"Oh Lata! I can never thank you enough for this" exclaimed Radha.

It was not long before Magan arrived and Radha hurried with him to the palace.

Radha entered the mighty walls of the Agra fort with the excitement and enthusiasm of a child. This was where her father came to work everyday she thought. They had entered from the western gate of the fort which was closer to the kitchen. Magan was carrying a letter of permission for Radha with the seal of the head cook. The guards looked at Radha before looking at the seal and then let her pass.

"The letter allows her only for a day. You cannot bring her with you tomorrow", said one of the guards. Magan nodded his head while Radha hurried behind him, trying to match up to his fast steps. She could hear the early morning Azaan from the mosque in the fort. They hardly met anyone on the way.

The Royal kitchen resembled a mini fortress inside the fort. Radha had never seen such humongous pots and pans and ladles. The kitchen was divided into vegetarian and non-vegetarian sections. The Emperor had lately started preferring vegetarian food. There were exotic vegetables and fruits from all parts of the Empire. Some lay in sacks and some on the shelves. There were crimson red apples and pink peaches from the Himalayan valleys of which Radha had heard so much. Radha feasted her eyes on the riot of colours and tried to memorise the picture for her next painting. Magan put a sack of potatoes before her to be peeled. Radha looked around for a suitable companion to pick up a conversation. She did not need to look too far. Before she realised, a young girl, almost her age, came to her. Piqued with curiousity she said, "I have never seen you here before".

"Yes, I have come here for the first time with my uncle Magan in place of the help who is on leave, but just for a day", replied Radha with extra politeness.

"Oh! I have been working here for the last six months. My mother is the parlour maid to the Hindu Queen. Have you heard of the Emperor's Hindu Queen? She was previously the princess of Amer. She has such long dark tresses. She loves to get it braided and decked up with jewels like they were done for her in Amer. My mother is an expert in the art."

While the girl rattled on with her stories about her mother and the Queen, Radha was quietly thanking her stars. She had been worried about how to pass on Suraj's message to some one close to the Emperor, as Suraj had directed her, and here she came across someone who had contact with the Queen.

"I have heard the Queen has beautiful paintings and murals in her chamber", Radha interrupted her companion's commentary, as she paused for breath in between.

"Oh yes! You have to see them to appreciate their beauty. They are life like. Almost ready to speak to you", she replied.

This gullible girl is heaven sent thought Radha.

"Please can you show them to me. Painting is my hobby and while coming here today I was secretly hoping to see the paintings of Radha and Krishna that adorn the Hindu Queen's chambers", said Radha.

The girl, whose name was Laxmi, was more than happy to hear this. Radha realized that relentless chatting was her nature and in Radha she had found a companion of the same age after a long time.

"I usually go to meet my mother after finishing my work here. That is mostly by late afternoon. Take permission from your uncle and you can come with me", she said.

Radha wasted no time in seeking Magan's permission. "Can I go to the Hindu Queen's palace with Laxmi. Her mother works there."

"But how can you enter the Queen's palace? No one will let you enter as you're a stranger here", said Magan.

"Laxmi says the Queen is resting at this hour and we will not enter her main palace. We will just see the paintings in the rooms outside where all her maids have access", replied Radha.

"You can try your luck Radha since that is the reason you came here, but be sure to be back well before sunset. You can easily get lost in the fort in the dark."

Radha promised Magan that she would be back well in time. Laxmi was already pulling her by the hand, impatient to take her to the Queen's palace. Magan however, did not let them leave till they both solemnly promised him again to be back as soon as possible.

Sixteen

THE ADVENTURE IN THE FORT

Today was the day Radha would remember as the most adventurous one in her life. She happily scampered along with Laxmi to the Queen's palace in the fort. It was a little walk from the kitchen. All along the way she kept checking the note from Suraj lest she should lose it. It was securely sewed in the folds of her dupatta.

"Will you be coming to help tomorrow too?", Laxmi asked her a second time.

"No, uncle has said that temporary replacements can only come for a day. A new helper the next day and so on till permanent one joins back or the post is filled up again. The rules of the Emperor are very strict. Especially after there have been instances of poisoning his food," replied Radha.

"Oh! How I wish you could come again", exclaimed Laxmi. "I have no girl of my age to talk to. It gets boring in the kitchen."

Radha and Laxmi were now at the entrance of the Hindu Queen Heera Kunwari's palace. Radha's keen artist's eye was quickly absorbing as much as she could. The entrance of the palace was guarded by two stout eunuchs.

"Laxmi, who is this pretty young girl with you today?", asked one of them and winked.

"She is from the kitchen. She came with her uncle today in place of Gafur who has been taken ill suddenly", replied Laxmi. "I am taking her with me to visit Ma. She wants to have a look at the Krishna paintings of the palace."

"Who are you to take her inside? We won't let her enter the palace", said the other and both started to laugh.

Radha felt uncomfortable for the first time since she had entered the fort. There was something formidable about the eunuchs.

"No one can enter the kitchen without a strict screening daily. You are welcome to frisk her again. She's an artist you see, just interested in the paintings. She's not here to steal something", said Laxmi trying her best to show her authority to Radha.

"Let's see how the young thing feels like", chuckled the eunuchs.

Radha flinched as the eunuchs groped her. She prayed they wouldn't feel the letter which was written on a cloth sewed to her dupatta. She slowly let go of her breath when they missed it. Lady Luck is definitely favoring me today, thought Radha. If I don't deliver Suraj's message today, I won't get another chance.

"Come come my girls. Go and have a look at the outer chambers. But come back here when the gong sounds four. That's the time the Queen gets up. Don't dare go anywhere near her personal chamber Laxmi, even if to meet your mother or else I will have to drag you out", said one of the eunuchs.

Laxmi caught hold of Radha's hand and ran away from them.Radha was lagging behind trying to assimilate the grand surroundings.

"Amma, see I have found a friend in the kitchen", Laxmi shouted on seeing her mother. Her mother, Kangan, was selecting flowers for the Queen's hair and motioned her to lower her voice.

"The Queen will be getting up soon. I have to go and style her hair now. I will talk to you and your friend later. Go back to the kitchen soon", replied her mother as she walked away.

"I promised Radha that I would show Radha the beautiful murals in the Queen's chamber", sulked Laxmi.

"Not inside her private chamber Laxmi. No one is allowed there except her personal maids and the

Emperor. You both can have a look outside here", said her mother.

Radha was suddenly nervous. Laxmi's mother would soon be gone and so would be the opportunity to send across Suraj's message.

Radha took Laxmi to a side and spoke fast, "Laxmi, you are a heaven sent blessing to me. I have a very important message to deliver to the Queen. If it is delayed not one but two lives will be in danger. I beg of you, convince your mother to pass on the message to the Queen and ask her to read it urgently."

Laxmi was astounded but recovered soon. Her sense of importance and the desire to prove her friendship to Radha took the better of her. She rushed to her mother at once with the little piece of cloth in which the message was written.

The Emperor's Hindu Queen Heera Kunwari, previously princess of Amer, woke up from her afternoon siesta. Her dark eyes gazed around the room looking for her favourite companion and maid since childhood, Gulabi. As if on cue Gulabi was just entering the room with a glass of water cooled in earthen pots. She handed it over to the Queen who sipped it slowly.

"Gulabi, it has been three days since the Emperor has visited us. Very soon he will leave for the hunt. Send a message that I would like to meet him tonight."

"Yes Heera, the message will be sent. But I hear that the hunt has been postponed because Hawai is not well."

"I want my hair to be washed and dried before the Emperor arrives. Call Kangan", ordered the Queen getting up from the bed.

Gulabi went out and told the maid standing outside the Queen's private room to bring in Kangan immediately.

Very soon Kangan entered the room, far from her normal self. She bowed before the Queen and went to the bath chamber to prepare for the Queen's head bath. The Queen entered and lay down in the cushioned bathtub while Kangan worked on her hair. After washing her hair she wrapped it up in a dry towel and waited for the Queen to be seated before the mirror. Long and thick incense sticks of sandalwood and jasmine were already burning. While Kangan combed the Queen's hair gently Gulabi held out one of the burning sticks close to her hair. Together Kangan and Gulabi worked slowly on the Queen's long hair. The Queen, enjoying the ritual, preferred to be quiet. Kangan wanted Gulabi to leave. "I need some more incense sticks" she told Gulabi. Gulabi left in search of more sticks.

"Kangan, is something on your mind. Ever since you've come today you are not your normal self", the Queen asked and looked at Kangan in the mirror.

"Begum Sahiba, I do have something on my mind. I am at a loss as to how to tell you", Kangan whispered nervously.

The Queen turned around to face Kangan. "Tell me quick. I do not have much time. I have to get ready before the Emperor arrives."

"A girl came in the kitchen today in place of a help who was ill. She came to your palace with my daughter Laxmi. Just as I was about to enter your chamber Laxmi passed me this message which the girl had handed over to her. She says its very urgent and must reach the Emperor without delay", Kangan said nervously.

The Queen extended her hand, "Show me the letter". Kangan handed over the little piece of cloth. The Queen read it quietly, her face betraying no emotion.

"Send a message to the kitchen at once. Who is this girl delivering a message to the Emperor in such a mysterious way. I don't want her to leave the fort", ordered the Queen.

A frightened Kangan ran out to convey the Queen's message to the eunuchs. The Queen's sat in pensive silence while Kangan continued her task of drying her hair slowly but meticulously. Kangan was petrified by the turn of events and could not utter a word.

"Why did you entertain a stranger in my palace Kangan?", asked the Queen after some time.

"I was caught unaware Begum Sahiba. Before I knew Laxmi had thrust the letter in my hands saying that it was imperative that it should reach the Emperor", replied Kangan.

"What is taking them so long to bring the girl", the Queen mused loudly.

Kangan was too scared to reply.

In the kitchen, Radha was whisked away by the two eunuchs. A shocked Magan was not even given time to question them as Radha disappeared before his eyes.

✪✪✪✪✪✪

Seventeen

AN EVENING OF SUSPENSE

Suraj waited impatiently beneath the window. The window was shut today. The shut window was not a good sign. It meant Radha was not in her room. If he continued pacing in the street he would be noticed sooner or later. Though it was well after sunset there was enough moonlight to make him visible. He decided to climb up the tree and see for himself. The window was fastened shut and there was no reflection of a lamp burning inside. Had Radha slept early today? But she slept with the window open. He was sure of that. Was she still in the courtyard or having dinner with her parents? He decided to wait for her a little longer, feeling like a thief, an imposter.

On hindsight, that was precisely what he had behaved like. Like a thief he had entered her room the previous nights, without her knowledge or permission. His anxiety grew with the darkness and silence around him. He decided to return in the morning. Although he had a very strong desire to knock at her door and inquire about her, he had to resist it. It would complicate things further. Wherever she was, he was sure that she was safe.

He decided to go back to the Sarai. The owner had several contacts in the city. There was always enough gossip among the drunken travelers to catch any significant development. For the first time, the gravity of involving Radha in his affairs hit him. When he looked back at the events of the past three days they seemed like a bad dream. Nothing had worked according to plan. His association with Hasan, Hasan's murder, landing up in Radha's room; it was like he was in a deep sleep and events were occuring without his control. He wished he woke up a happy man.

He had reached the Sarai. He was tired of walking as it was a long way from Radha's house. Wearily, he climbed the steps to the owner's room. "Any news from the fort?", he asked as soon as he met the owner.

The owner was surprised. "You look tense Suraj. Is anything the matter?", he asked Suraj. He had not told him about confiding in Radha and asking her for help. Suraj decided it was necessary to tell him the whole truth if he expected assistance from him. He briefly told him about the strange coincidences that had led to his meeting Radha more than once and her willingness to help. The owner's astonishment was visible on his face as he heard Suraj's strange story.

"You trusted a girl who's father is a faithful employee of Todar Mal, who himself is quite close to the Emperor? You have known her for hardly two days? I am surprised at your naivety Suraj. It is quite unlike you", said the owner.

"So am I", replied Suraj almost to himself. It was not that he doubted Radha. He knew she was an honest girl and would not deceive him, but he was repenting her involvement. Perhaps lack of food and sleep and the constant running had dulled his sharp brains. Otherwise he would have thought of another way out.

"Can you send someone to the fort to find out about her? If there is no news of her till morning, I will have to go the fort myself", said Suraj.

"Give me some time. I have a contact in the court who is expected around midnight. Let us see if he has any information. If not, we'll plan something. We can send someone to her house early in the morning tomorrow under some pretence and find out if she has reached home safely", the owner said.

Suraj agreed. The owner had excellent judgement and could always be relied upon.

"I'm sure she is safe wherever she is. You try to catch some sleep."

Suraj knew it was impossible to sleep. He left the inn immediately and started walking towards the river. It was a long walk. He reached the shore and sat under the same Neem tree. He followed the constellations he followed at home. The moon was nearly full, in the waning phase. The same moon would be visible in Chittor. How he wished to see it from the rooftop of his house right now.

He thought of Radha and the thought pained him. He was missing her company and wanted to be near her wherever she was.

Unaware of Suraj's thoughts dwelling on her, Radha had been whisked away to meet the Queen. Everything had happened so suddenly that Radha was feeling numb. The eunuchs had strong, rough hands and were putting too much pressure on her elbows. Her first concern at the moment was not about herself but how Magan would break the news of her absence to her parents. What would her father do if he came to know about her? The thought made her shudder. Had she been foolish to trust Suraj? What evidence did she have that he was speaking the truth? She was surprised at herself that even now she did not doubt his honesty. So much so that she did not even bother to read the message he was sending through her and had just repeated the words he had told her to.

She now stood before the Queen while Laxmi's mother dried out her tresses. The Queen did not turn around to look at her but saw her reflection in the mirror. Her manner appeared haughty, as a Queen's should be, thought Radha. Radha kept standing, waiting for the Queen to speak but there was total silence. A peacock screamed somewhere in the garden outside. After sometime the Queen turned around and asked for the eunuchs and Kangan to leave her alone with Radha. Radha looked at the ground, shying from looking at the Queen in her face. The Queen studied Radha for a while. Radha felt a sense of relief in the absence of the eunuchs. Her elbows were still aching.

"What is your name?", asked the Queen.

"Radha, she replied still gazing at the floor."

"And who is your Krishna for whom you entered the fort with such extra-ordinary courage to pass on his message?"

Radha was taken aback. Did the Queen know about Suraj? She immediately looked up at the Queen. The first thing she noticed in her beautiful face were her dark and benevolent eyes. Radha new the truth was too far fetched to be believed. Yet, she had no other story to tell. She was too simple to fabricate a false one.

"I do not know him at all Begum Sahiba. He was injured and just happened to find shelter in my home. He says if he enters the fort he is sure to be arrested and killed. His sincerity and distress appealed to my conscience. He wanted me to deliver this message to someone really close to the Emperor and I agreed", Radha spoke fast but clearly.

The Queen smiled to herself. Her guess had been right. She was doing this for love after all, without knowing it herself. What else can lead to such blind faith.

Aloud she said, "You do not seem so unintelligent as you have behaved. Do you know the enormity of this message?"

"Begum Sahiba will not believe me I'm sure but I have not laid my eyes upon the message", Radha whispered.

The improbability of the whole scheme was now dawning upon Radha. The Queen was now smiling openly.

"I believe you. Your name is Radha. You cannot be wrong. Though your Krishna might be", she said and smiled.

Radha stood quietly, not knowing what to say.

The Queen went on, "The content of this letter if true cannot be dealt with lightly. I will call Assad Khan, the head of the Royal secret service and hand over the matter to him. Until then you cannot leave the palace. Don't worry, you are safe here."

Radha could not believe that the letter had finally reached the person it was intended for. At the same time, the immediate prospect of not being able to return home for the night made Radha very nervous. As if reading her thoughts, the Queen tried to calm her down.

"Don't worry. The cook who brought you here will convey your whereabouts to your parents".

"My father is an officer in the court. He works for Raja Todar Mal", Radha managed to say despite her confusion. "He has no knowledge about the reason I'm here".

"What reason did you give at home for coming to the fort?", asked an amused Queen.

"I am an amateur painter. I told my uncle who works in the kitchen that I was interested in the paintings of the fort. To my mother I lied that I was visiting my best friend's house", replied Radha, now close to tears.

"We will not mention anything about the message to the cook. I will tell him that I want you to draw a fine painting of Radha and Krishna for me and so am keeping you for the night."

Radha's face lit up with relief. Tears of gratitude welled up in her eyes. Though her parents would be worried they would at least know she was safe. She promised to herself never to hide anything from them again.

✪✪✪✪✪✪

Eighteen

THE INTERVIEW

Assad Khan read the letter for the third time. He was glad the Queen had handed it over directly to him and not involved the Emperor in the affair. She had proved again that she was wiser than the other Queens. The only way to know the complete truth was from the person who had written it. The Queen had told him that the bearer of the letter was a young girl who had risked a lot to deliver it. Somehow he felt that the Queen was reluctant to allow him to interview the girl.

He had insisted and promised that he would interview her from behind the curtain.

"She's brave but she's very nervous right now. I don't think she has anything to do with the matter except that she happened to give shelter to the fugitive without knowing that he was a fugitive from the fort", the Queen had told him.

Assad Khan was an astute judge of character. All he needed was an interview with this girl and he would be able to sieve out a few falsehoods for himself. Right now he needed to give his undivided attention to the strange letter. Now that he had read and re-read the letter he decided to interview the girl. The Queen sent a message that the girl was ready to be interviewed. When the attendant informed him that the Queen was ready to receive him in her personal chamber he left immediately. He entered the Queen's chamber for the second time today and was yet again impressed by her. Beautiful in her majestic Rajputana way, yet fiercely independent. Even the Emperor was intimidated by her sense of independence. She was proud of her Suryavanshi lineage and had refused to be converted to Islam, though she respected it. She knew nothing about this girl's background but she immediately felt responsible for her. It were these qualities that made her stand tall among the other Queens.

"She is standing behind the curtain, you can start the interview", the Queen said without wasting time as soon as Assad Khan entered.

"Who gave you this letter?"

"A young man who calls himself Suraj".

Assad Khan was confused. He had thought that the Rajput's name was Chandan. Maybe he was using an alias. Maybe he was playing mind games with them. It was difficult to understand his motives.

"How do you know him?"

"He entered my room in a injured condition without my knowledge two nights before. And then he again took refuge in my room the night after that", Radha replied.

"Such a short acquaintance and you are ready to take the risk of delivering his message?", inquired Assad Khan.

"The circumstances under which I met him and the strange coincidence of meeting him again and again led me to believe him. He was a stranger in the city and desperate for help. I found him honest and was ready to help him".

Radha then repeated in details her meetings with Suraj. Assad Khan did not interrupt her while she told her story. Radha had decided to stick to the truth as much as possible. After she had finished he spoke.

"I want you to go back and call Suraj to the palace. That is the only way he can avoid arrest".

Radha was more than eager to go back home. Whether she would meet Suraj again or not she did not know. She also knew by now Suraj would be worried for her. Would it be wise to tell him to come to the palace? That was for him to decide she thought. She had done her job and wanted to leave the fort as soon as possible.

"I would do that as soon as I get a chance to meet him. It is not necessary that I meet him again", replied Radha truthfully.

"He will come to meet you. Of that I'm sure", replied Assad Khan from experience.

"It is very late in the night. You can go home tomorrow morning. Remember to convey to him the message that he can come and meet me without any fear."

Radha exhaled a deep breath. It was only when her body relaxed that she realised how tense she had been.

Laxmi took Radha to her mother's quarters in the fort to spend the night with them.

Three days had passed since Hasan's murder. The messengers and soldiers sent out in search of the Rajput called Chandan alias Suraj, had drawn flak. Now that he had some lead about the horse trainer, Assad Khan had a clear plan of action. The pieces of the jigsaw puzzle that were strewn far apart were now slowly falling into place. He was sure that the Rajput was still in Agra though his subordinates tried to convince him that he had left for Chittor. Assad Khan thought otherwise. Why send a message to the Emperor if he had plans of fleeing? He was eager to meet this young man called Chandan or Suraj. His hopes were pinned on the girl who had delivered the message so daringly. He was also expecting Haider Khan to bring some news from Mehrunissa that might throw some more light on the mystery surrounding Hasan's death. He hoped that Haider Ali had questioned her thoroughly. He knew that being Hasan's close companion she would have been more frank with Haider. When he had met her she seemed hesitant to talk about Hasan. Maybe Hasan had shared something about the Rajput that she would confide in Haider. He continued to pace his chamber impatiently. He had a few more people to interview regarding the murder. When there was no news from Haider, he set about his task.

There was still no new development in the case by evening. Assad Khan ordered that Haider Khan be conveyed the message that he wanted to meet him urgently. The reply was immediate. Haider was already on his way to meet the Chief.

"I have been waiting for you all day hoping you would bring some news from Mehrunissa", said Assad Khan as soon as Haider Ali entered his chamber.

"I had gone to meet her in the afternoon to avoid her husband. But he informed me that she was not at home and was expected in the evening. I thought that if I went there again today it would make him suspicious. So I've decided to go again in the morning tomorrow." replied Haider. "Meanwhile I've continued with my inquiries about the horse-trainer.The Chief recruiter of horse trainers, Hari Dass seems unduly fond of him. I think we should probe him further. He might be lying. He might know his whereabouts", he continued.

Assad Khan continued pacing the room without slackening his speed. The sun had set on another day. Though a clear picture was emerging from the haze of the past two days, the face of the culprit was still not clear. He could not write off the Rajput as the assailant yet. This could all be a well thought out plan with far reaching implications on the Emperor's relation with Mewar. The coincidences were many. The morning would make the picture clearer he was sure.

He looked at Haider. He was looking tired and older. The past three days had been hard on him too.

"Is there any news of the Rajput?" he asked Assad Khan.

"No, neither from Agra nor from Chittor. We had even sent a few messengers to Ajmer where his family lives. No news of him from there too", replied Assad Khan. Both men fell silent. Assad Khan had decided not to tell anyone about the girl's message for the time being. He wanted to keep it a secret as long as possible. He was sure the Rajput boy would come to meet her.

"The Emperor is preparing to leave for the Qumargah tomorrow. Hawai is back in good form. Hari Dass will accompany the Emperor, so it is better that you meet him today", Haider Khan said.

"Yes, I know. He must be busy today with the horses that are going for the hunt. I will go and meet him myself", replied the Chief of the spy services.

"Good night Sir. I will meet Mehrunissa tomorrow morning and report to you immediately after", said Haider and wished him good bye. Assad Khan walked slowly towards the area of the fort which housed the horses of the nobles who would accompany the Emperor in his hunting expedition. He was hoping that Hari Dass would still be at work. On reaching the stables he was informed that he had left early today and would be back early next morning.

"Everything has to be postponed for tomorrow morning it seems", thought Assad Khan and returned to his quarters.

✪✪✪✪✪✪

Ninteen

AN EVENTFUL DAY

Radha could not sleep. Laxmi was excited about the whole incident and had a lot of questions to ask her, but her mother would not let her to talk to Radha. Radha waited for the first rays of the sun to appear. As soon as it was dawn, the fort gates would open and she could leave.

The chirping of the birds was almost synchronous with the morning 'Azaan'. Suraj woke up. He was feeling sore after spending the night under the tree. Though he had meant to go back to the inn, he had fallen asleep under the stars. The rays of the rising sun weaved golden magic over the waters of Yamuna. Birds who had come back to their nests in the evening , were making noise as they flew out of their homes to look for food. Suraj sat for a while under the tree, looking at the rising sun. He decided to reach the inn before the city was awake and about. From where he stood he could see the southern gate of the Agra fort. The inn was in the opposite direction. Suddenly he felt like taking a detour to Radha's house, which was closer to the western gate, and check on her. Her house was not far from the fort. As he crossed the western gate he saw two figures walking ahead of him. He tried to close the distance between himself and the two. One looked like a soldier and the other was a girl. It was still not bright enough to make them out clearly. But the girls height and gait confirmed she was Radha. Suraj now decided to maintain some distance from them. He did not want any more complications.

He followed them without losing sight of them. This meant that Radha had spent the night in the fort. He could hardly wait to talk to her. The soldier walked a little behind Radha as she led the way. He looked like a eunuch. Soon they reached her house. Radha knocked at the main door. The door opened and she disappeared from his sight. The soldier stood there for a while speaking and then turned back. He was indeed a eunuch.Suraj did not wait any longer. He had already taken a different route. It would be a long one but he'd still reach the inn in time. While on one hand it was a relief to see Radha being escorted home, on the other he could hardly wait to talk to her. He did not want to take any chances right now. Like always he would wait for the night to fall.He hoped the window of her room would be open tonight.

He entered the inn with a lighter heart than he had left it. He ordered breakfast and ate alone. The owner was in his room as usual. The servant boy told Suraj that he was awake and wanted to talk to him. Suraj went up to his room and told him about Radha.

"The search for you has intensified Suraj. The Emperor's soldiers had come here last night. It was a stroke of luck that you were not here. Your disguise is practically of no use. They had a very good likeness of you, both with and without the beard. You have to remain here till we leave for Chittor as soon as possible", the owner said as he paced the room.

"I have to meet the girl at night. I'm sure she has a message for me. It is only after meeting her that we can decide on our future course of action", replied Suraj.

"Staying here is inviting arrest and imminent torture. By now they must have traced that you came from Chittor and will show no mercy in your treatment after the arrest", said the owner.

"Be assured. I have not the least intention to be arrested by them. I also feel that it is best to leave the city as early as possible. Let me meet Radha tonight and I will do as you say", replied Suraj anxiously.

The owner still had his doubts. "I would prefer that we leave immediately. I will change your appearance to that of an old man. We can leave right now", said the owner.

"You help me change my appearance. But I have to meet the girl. She went to the fort because I convinced her to. It's imperative that I meet her. I will go to meet her incognito as an old man." Suraj managed to convince the owner of the Sarai.

The owner gave in to Suraj's adamancy. He new he would never leave without meeting Radha. He set about to work immediately. He had to think of a foolproof plan which would help Suraj meet Radha and yet not let him get caught. It was a tough task but the inn-owner loved challenges.

✪✪✪✪✪✪

Twenty

ANOTHER SLEEPLESS NIGHT

Radha had a welcome that she had expected. As soon as she entered home she found Lata weeping silently in a corner. Her mother waited for the eunuch who had escorted her home to be safely out of hearing range, and then vented out all the anger that she had been piling up since Radha's escapade. Her father looked at her silently with one of the gravest expressions she had ever seen on his gentle face.

"If you had such a burning desire to visit the fort, why plan it secretly with Lata? Could you not have simply asked your father?", her mother shouted.

Radha could have explained that she had asked her father twice before but she chose to remain silent. She knew she deserved every bit of her mother's harsh words because she had actually betrayed her parents' confidence. More than her mother's outburst it was her father's silence that was deafening. She wanted to apologise and ask for forgiveness but knew that it would sound shallow.

Meanwhile her mother continued, "Why are you standing like a statue ? Didn't I tell you this girl will give us sleepless nights? You should have married her off last year when the proposal from Delhi had come. It was such a rich family. She would not have had time for such misadventures there."

Her father spoke up cutting her mother short, "Why did the Queen want you to spend the night in the palace?"

"She got interested when I told her that I do Radha and Krishna paintings. She wanted me to paint a scene she had in her mind for long. I spent most of the night painting." Radha felt relieved after speaking to her father, though she had to lie about the night.

"Go to your room now", he said. Lata will bring you something to eat."

"Amma, Baba, I'm sorry. I'll never again leave home without informing you as long as I live." Saying these words Radha ran up to the solace of her room and burst into tears as soon as she lay on her bed. She cried herself to sleep. When she woke up around noon, her mother was standing with a plate of food next to her bed.

"I have been trying to wake you up for some time. Get up now and eat something."

Radha sat up in bed and took the plate from her mother's hand. Her mother sat beside her while Radha ate in silence.

After Radha had finished her meal, her mother lovingly stroked her hair, asked her to have a bath and left the room..

Radha busied herself for the remaining hours and waited for night to fall. She prayed that Suraj would come and meet her one last time. She did not want to involve herself in his problems any more. She knew that her mother's suspicions had been aroused. She hoped Suraj would enter her room unnoticed like before.

Suraj, on the other hand was not so keen for the night. He was convinced now that Radha's house was no longer a safe place. It would be surrounded by spies. He could not risk going there any more. He had to think of some other means of communicating with her. He trusted the owner's presence of mind and decided to consult him.

"I would still advise that you leave Agra. This city is no longer safe for you." said the owner.

"They need me now more than ever. Radha has delivered only the partial truth. They cannot harm me because only I know the complete truth. I don't want to be a prisoner in the fort either. I desperately want to meet Radha and know what message she brings from them. Going to her house would be foolish. I'm sure her house in under watch now that they know exactly where she lives. That was the very reason for escorting her to her house today morning. Even going in a disguise as we had planned earlier would be dangerous", said Suraj hopelessly.

The owner was busy thinking. "Don't worry Suraj. I have a plan. It'll work", he said patting Suraj on his shoulders.

✪✪✪✪✪✪

Twenty One

ANOTHER MURDER

Assad Khan woke up in a defiant mood. He had to take a few important decisions today. Last night his men had come back empty handed from Radha's house. The Rajput had again managed to elude them. Not a single soul was seen in the vicinity of her house in the morning, afternoon, evening or night except for their maid who left late in the evening. The spies had worked in shifts and it was impossible that they would have fallen asleep and missed someone suspicious. The only person who came to the doorstep late in the evening, was a messenger from the court for her father, who did not even enter the house.

Assad Khan was now sure that the Rajput had communicated to Radha through this man who had dressed up as a court messenger and fooled the spies. The Rajput had again outwitted them. He was always a step ahead of them. Yet he was convinced of his presence in Agra. The first thing that he wanted to do today was to meet Mehrunissa. He had a very strong intuition that she knew much more than she had told him. He did not wait for Haider and decided to meet her himself. Early morning would be the best time to catch her at home. He did not care if her husband was at home. It was too late to observe formalities now. He was just about to leave when the guard announced that Haider Khan wanted to meet him urgently.

"Send him in", said Assad Khan adjusting his turban. An agitated Haider entered the room. Assad Khan knew something was definitely wrong.

"What is it?", he asked.

"I have just returned from Mehrunissa's house. There was a crowd outside as I approached her house. On inquiring, I came to know that she was dead and her body was found on the banks of the Yamuna, not far from her house last evening. She had been slit on the neck just like Hasan. When she did not return home last evening,her husband with a couple of his friends went out looking for her. They found her lying dead, close to the riverbank", said Haider in one breath.

"Someone must have wanted to dump the body in the river but possibly did not get enough time to do so", Assad Khan replied, but his thoughts were far away. It was a double murder now. He had to meet the Emperor.

"I wish you had been able to meet Mehrunissa before the tragedy struck. Maybe she would have been alive today. Maybe...." was all he said to Haider.

"Thank you for informing me immediately. I have a busy day ahead. I have to meet the Emperor before he leaves for the hunt", he said to Haider as he left his chamber.

Haider was eager to leave too.

"Hari Dass, the Chief recruiter of horse trainers is still missing. His room has not been slept in. I have a feeling that he might be with the absconding Rajput", Haider said before taking leave.

"I will personally look into the matter Haider. The culprit will be in the dungeons of the Agra fort before the sun sets on the Yamuna today", replied Assad Khan and bade Haider good bye.

He put on his sash and took his sword and asked his messenger to seek an interview with the the Emperor urgently. Meanwhile he left his chambers and walked slowly towards the rooms of Hari Dass.

At the other end of the town, the Sarai's owner had not yet returned. Suraj was waiting for him restively. The man who had been to Radha's house dressed up as a messenger from the court from had done his job well. He has been able to lure Radha's mother and then Radha to come out and receive the message from the Hindu Queen. Seeking an opportune moment he had asked Radha if she had any message for Suraj. Radha was stunned into silence first. He had then gone on to assure her that he had been sent by Suraj since it was dangerous for him to visit her now. Radha then told him that Suraj's message had been delivered successfully but to verify its truthfulness, Suraj would have to present himself before the Chief of the Royal spy services as soon as it was possible for him.

Suraj wished he could have thanked Radha in person and shown his gratitude for her unconditional support. He knew that whatever he said would sound less in front of her magnanimity. The owner had been present when the man posing as Queen's messenger had come back with Radha's message. In the present conditions Suraj trusted the owner's common sense more than his own. Between the two of them they decided to enter the fort at night and once there, request to meet Assad Khan. The owner had insisted on accompanying Suraj and Suraj had agreed out of sheer lack of the will to argue. He hoped that even if he was held captive, the owner would be let free to convey the the tidings to Rana Udai Singh in Chittor. The owner was away for some last minute preparations before their final entry into the enemy's territory.

Unknown of the developments, Radha could hardly eat or sleep normally. She had hoped fervently that Suraj would pay her one last visit at night. The message he had sent through his man had thrashed any such hopes. It was only then that she had realized that her house was under constant watch and admired Suraj for his foresightedness. Now that his entry into the fort was close she felt a sense of dread and gloom settle on her. Would she ever meet Suraj again? Would he be captured by the Mughals or would he be free to return to Chittor? She did not see any chance of meeting him either way. She heaved a sigh and got up to finish her landscape. Why did he have to enter her room that night she thought. If it was destined that they should meet, then they would meet again for sure. The thought brightened her and she stopped brooding over Suraj. She immersed herself into her painting.

✪✪✪✪✪✪

Twenty Two

ASSAD KHAN MEETS THE EMPEROR

The young Jallaluudin could no longer hide his excitement for the hunt. Hawai's illness had delayed it for a week. When the guard announced the arrival of Assad Khan early in the morning, his sixth sense was quick to discern that something was definitely not right. Assad Khan entered his private chamber and saluted him customarily. Akbar was carefully cleaning his newly acquired prized possession-the musket he called Sangram. He would be testing it for the first time in the hunt.

"Something sinister?", asked the Emperor.

"Another bid at your life Emperor, at least I think so", replied Assad Khan.

"Bring in the culprit. Let me test Sangram on him. If he escapes, his good luck", chuckled the young Emperor aiming his latest toy at an imaginary culprit.

"The identity of the culprit is a mystery Jahanpanah. The person we had all along believed to be the culprit is the one who has revealed the plan of the attempt on your life", replied Assad Khan.

"Bring in this fellow. Let me have the plan that has been hatched for my speedy departure from this world straight from the horse's mouth", replied the Emperor still unperturbed.

"We have been trying to trace him for the last three days since one of my boys Hasan was found murdered."

The Emperor finally put away his musket and sat down. Assad Khan knew that behind his nonchalance, he had guessed the urgency of the situation. He quickly related the events of the past few days.

"And this message that the Rajput sent says that the plot to have me killed has been hatched in my own palace?", the Emperor said.

"Yes, Jahanpanah. But he will reveal the names of the persons involved only on meeting me", replied Assad Khan.

"Wait for him then. If he has conveyed the message he will definitely turn up and soon at that. I want you to bring him to me as soon he presents himself. After meeting him I shall proceed for the Qumargah. The beaters must have reached quite deep into the jungle by now. I cannot delay it any longer." Saying this the Emperor dismissed Assad Khan.

Assad Khan knew that Queen Heera Kunwari had already informed the Emperor about the message. He also knew that the Emperor was aware of his knowledge of the fact. But this common knowledge was kept out of the conversation. The Emperor was famous for not mentioning any of his Queens while discussing matters of the court with his officers. Assad Khan respected him for this and so he did not mention the Queen's involvement in the affair either.

He was well aware that the Emperor had an idea of the entire situation beforehand but did not interrupt him as he wanted an official account. He already felt lighter now that he had shared the information with him.

His next halt was Mehrunissa's house. Her sudden, tragic end had created an atmosphere of gloom well palpable outside her house. He requested the same maid, who had waited on him previously to send a message of his arrival to Mir Qazi. The Qazi appeared instantly. He was older than Assad Khan with a long grey beard which he kept stroking at surprisingly regular intervals. He looked at Assad Khan with undisguised interest. Assad Khan could not detect any trace of mourning on his face.

"I am Assad Khan. Chief of the Royal spy service. I have come to meet you regarding the untimely demise of your wife. Please accept my condolences."

Mir Qazi first grunted then stroked his beard. "She died just like that slimy lover of hers. Murdered in cold blood. Slit on the neck."

Assad Khan was taken aback at the harsh words. It was almost as if he killed them both. "Had he?", thought Assad Khan. The way things were turning he was open to all possibilities. It was obvious that there was not much love lost between the husband and his dead wife.

"I knew you had come inquiring about him after his death. You should have come to me. I knew everything about them", Mir Qazi continued with another stroke of his beard. "Perhaps it was my fault. I married a woman half my age, hoping to have a son that my previous wife could not gift me. Anyways now that she is gone, that chapter is closed forever". He sighed.

"Who do you think could be behind the murders?" Assad Khan asked directly.

"That is your job to find out, is it not? You are paid handsomely for it. It is clear that the same person who killed Hasan Ali is behind this. She knew something that she was afraid to tell anyone. The day she left, it was to meet you or someone she trusted. But fate had other plans", he said and got up from the Diwan on which he had been siting.

"You have no idea what it was that she wanted to tell?" probed Assad Khan quietly as he also stood up.

The Qazi stroked his beard and shook his head in the negative.

"I shall not disturb you any longer. I am grateful to you for taking out time for me in this hour of grief. Please accept my condolences once again."

Assad Khan left with a brisk turn having gained nothing new from the interview except for the Qazi's hatred for his wife and Hasan and a possible motive for murder. He had hoped to reach nearer to the end of the mystery surrounding Hasan's death but now he was returning to the fort with added confusions. Mir Qazi could easily be responsible for both deaths. Was he unnecessarily linking Hasan's death with the Rajput?

✪✪✪✪✪✪

Twenty Three

A MUCH AWAITED MEETING

The keeper of the inn returned just as it started to get dark.

"Are you ready Suraj ?" He asked

"Whenever you are", replied Suraj.

"Good. Let us have a light dinner and leave".

They both ate in the room above to avoid the travelers below. They did not take long to eat as both of them were in a hurry to leave. Having finished eating they both dressed their heads in their traditional turbans. The keeper took his personal sword which was hanging on the wall and gave Suraj another one. Before leaving the keeper called out to one of his helpers and took him aside. They had a brief conversation before finally leaving the inn.

"What did you tell him?", asked Suraj.

"I have instructed him to instantly leave for Mewar in case we do not return till morning or sent him a message from the Agra fort."

Suraj nodded. The most difficult task at hand right now was to avoid being arrested on entering the enemy's fort. Last time he had entered as an employee with recommendations from Hasan. Today he would be entering as an imposter and a murder suspect. The inn keeper had insisted on accompanying him though Suraj had repeatedly warned him of the dangers that lay ahead.

"Two head strong Rajputs are enough to create a tumult in the fort", he had chuckled in reply. They decided to use horses to reach the fort. Two of their men were already waiting for them at a pre-decided spot near the fort. They handed over the horses to them.

The moment of truth had finally arrived for Suraj. They informed the guards at the western gates of the fort of their identity. They knew that their arrival was awaited. The guards lowered the bridge over the moat and Suraj with the inn keeper took their first step into the enemy's territory.

As Suraj had anticipated, the guards had been informed well in advance of their expected arrival. Assad Khan was unaware that, just like him, the Emperor was watching the gates from his watch tower. As soon as the two entered the fort, the Emperor beckoned a messenger and sent him to Assad Khan. Assad Khan was on his way to meet the Emperor when the messenger met him. Assad Khan was startled yet again at the young Emperor's foresight. Assad Khan had already instructed the guards at the gates to bring the Rajput to his chamber. He was not surprised that he was not alone. He secretly admired the Rajputs for their valor and conviction and this one was no exception. The messenger conveyed the Emperor's message to Assad Khan and walked away.

Meanwhile the two Rajputs were slightly taken aback at the warm reception. They were asked no questions when Suraj informed who he was. There was no attempt to take them captive. Even their swords were not asked for. The Mughals were not to be trusted, thought Suraj, more so if they acted friendly. Sensing the danger that was lurking in every corner of the fort, Suraj became even more wary.Unseen eyes were following their every movement. Suraj could almost feel the gazes. They were escorted to a chamber which was elegantly but sparsely decorated and there they were left alone. After waiting for what seemed a long time, they heard footsteps. Instinctively their hands went to their swords. Two men entered the room. An older one of around fifty and a younger one of around twenty five. Both looked like officials in the court. The older one introduced himself. "I am Assad Khan. I head the spy services of Emperor Jalaluddin. Who is the person who sent the message through the girl?"

Suraj spoke up "I had sent the message." Assad Khan looked at Suraj and his companion.

"Are you Chandan? Was it you that Hassan had recommended as a horse trainer?"

Suraj nodded. "My real name is Suraj. Yes, Hassan had met me in Chittor and had became a dear friend."

"Whether he was your friend or foe is questionable right now. How did you gain the information you passed in the message?"

"The story starts in Chittor", Suraj replied. Suraj began his tale which was stranger than fiction.

✪✪✪✪✪✪

Twenty Four

SURAJ'S NARRATIVE

"I met Hasan Ali in winter last year when he was in Chittor. The first time we met was when I was buying a horse from a trader who had come from Persia. Hasan Ali had a keen interest in horses and my conversation with the trader drew him towards me. We both started to talk about horses and connected with each other very comfortably. He told me that he had come to buy a couple of good horses for the Mughal Emperor and had information about the Persian trader's arrival in Chittor. My knowledge about horses fascinated him and I was in turn fascinated by his tales of Agra city. He was putting up at an inn and I invited him to say with me as I was staying alone in Chittor, my family being in Ajmer. I struck a good deal for him with the Persian trader.

While he was leaving I expressed my desire to work in the Mughal army as I needed money. He said that the cavalry would benefit much from a horse trainer like me and it was decided between the two of us that I would visit Agra when my work here was finished.

My real reason for visiting Agra was the same as was Hasan's for visiting Chittor as I would later come to know; to gain knowledge of the enemy's preparation for battle. At that point of time neither Hasan nor me were aware of each other's true identity or intentions, but we had forged a good friendship because we genuinely liked each other.

I am a close friend and confidante of Pratap Singh and the impending war of the Mughals against Mewar is common knowledge. When I had passingly mentioned about Hasan to Pratap, he had suggested that I make use of the opportunity. In fact when I was reluctant to work as a spy he told me that Hasan was doing the same job there in Chittor. I refused to believe him then but now I admire his far-sightedness. It was then decided that I would work in the Mughal army in summer and come back with first hand knowledge.

On reaching Agra I met my only contact here, Hasan Ali. We were both actually delighted to meet each other again. The very same day he took me to meet Hari Dass, the recruiter of horse- trainers. Like Hasan, he was soon impressed with my expertise on horses and recruited me immediately. Hasan's reference was enough for him. I was allotted a small quarter in the fort not far from the stables. The quarter had been empty for many years and required cleaning so I lodged with Hasan temporarily. Hasan had told me he worked in the court for the Emperor and mostly performed services for him outside of Agra. I did not probe him either about the exact nature of his job.

The next evening, thinking my room must be ready, I decided to go there to keep my few belongings. As I approached the room I overheard the conversation I had mentioned in the message. I was alerted by voices that I had not heard before, when I was reached the isolated quarters. They were two of them and their voices sounded young. They were discussing about the Emperor's upcoming hunt and how the slow poisoning of his elephant Hawai had been detected and had foiled their plans. One of them was blaming the other and seemed to be a man of authority. He then asked the other to leave no room for mistake in the hunt and aim for the poisoned arrow at the Emperor at the most suitable opportunity. No one would suspect him as he had already arranged for a stampede of animals at the last stage of the Qumargah. He said that the Emperor had made enough enemies for a lifetime and deserved to die. I concealed myself as well as possible and when they left the room I could clearly see their faces.

I found the incident strange and serious. I wanted to mention it to Hasan as soon as possible. No Emperor deserved a death of deceit is what Rajputs believe and their can be no greater cowardice than your own friend stabbing you in the back. Their treachery did not stop at this. What alarmed me the most was that if the Emperor died in the hunt they were planning to blame the poisoning of Hawai on a young Hindu boy who worked in the enclosure of Hawai. They were laughing about how they would link the attack on the Emperor to his arch rival Pratap Singh. It would be a blotch on the history of any Rajput to kill his enemy by deceit and treachery even if it was a lie. Even though untrue, it would still go down in history as the truth."

Assad Khan and his companion exchanged glances.

Suraj continued. "I wanted to meet Hasan at the first opportune moment. I went in search of him and finally found him as he was about to leave the fort. When I told him that I had an urgent matter to discuss with him, he said that we would discuss it in the morning. I told him that I would like to talk outside the fort and so we decided to meet early morning in the market place. Little did we know that the thick fort walls have ears too. The same evening as I left the fort for a stroll, I was followed and attacked. I was stabbed in the shoulder but fortunately the wound was not deep. The knife was aimed for the heart I guess but missed aim as I moved. I outwitted my attackers as they chased me and finally found refuge for the night in the house of the girl who delivered my message. The next morning I reached the market to meet Hasan as planned and I was followed there too. I tried to keep a step ahead of the person following me. Before there was a hue and cry about the murder I had already left the market oblivious of my friend's fate." Suraj stopped his narrative. It was some time before he resumed.

"When I came to know about Hasan I was sure that the prime suspicion would fall on me. That was the compelling reason that I continued to stay away from the fort and did not inform you about the sequence of events myself. I knew I would never be believed. A Rajput from Chittor, just a couple of days old in the city and with his only contact dead had little chances of justice. I am certain that even now if I tell you the name of the person who is scheming against your Emperor I will not be believed."

While Suraj was telling his story the owner of the Sarai did not change his position and stood with his feet slightly apart glaring at Assad Khan and his companion. He was a stout and tall man and his mere presence was intimidating to Assad Khan, but being in his own territory he was at ease. He finally spoke up.

"I have already guessed the name. It is Haider Khan."

The startled look on Suraj's face was enough to confirm that he was right.

✪✪✪✪✪✪

Twenty Five

ASSAD KHAN'S NARRATIVE

Suraj was stumped by Assad Khan. He had underestimated him just as Assad Khan had underestimated Suraj.

"The day your message arrived that the Emperor's life was at risk and someone amongst the court officials was involved I started ruling out all possibilities. I had always known that Hasan's murder was somehow linked to the Emperor. Your message confirmed it. Hawai's sudden change of temper and ill-health had cautioned me before hand that some foul play would occur during the hunt. I inquired into Hawai's diet and concluded that it was not possible to tamper with his diet except while he was actually feeding. I questioned his personal supervisors about the day Hawai fell ill. Surprisingly there was an interval of about ten to fifteen minutes when they were distracted from Hawai by an incident which though small, was big enough to draw my suspicion towards Haider. A lady had come to the feeding area and pleaded them to come and help feed her pet goat who was tethered nearby and had not eaten for a couple of days. This was the first time these two supervisors had laid eyes on the goat. They did not recognise the lady either but from her attire they knew she was a maid of some lady of the nobility. From their description of her I narrowed down to a few personal maids. I took these two boys to have a look at these maids surreptitiously. We finally picked up on Amna, the personal maid of Haider's wife. I was initially very surprised and was convinced that the boys had made a mistake. Haider was one of Hasan's closest and oldest friend and his involvement in his murder was remote. But could he be involved in tampering Hawai's food? I decided not to question Amna. It would raise Haider's suspicion and at that stage I felt I could be unwise. Instead, I decided to work backwards and traced Haider's history before he joined the court as a spy.

We always maintain a meticulous record of our employees. I was in for a shock. Haider Khan's other name in the records was Mukhtar Khan. He had not mentioned his parents name in the records but mentioned that they lived in Kabul. We traced his roots back to Kabul and came to know from our very reliable source in Kabul that he was actually the second of the four offsprings of Maham Anga. He had been left behind in Kabul while Maham Anga had travelled to India with the young Emperor and Adham Khan. Why had he kept this fact such a well guarded secret? Why did he have to impersonate as an ordinary spy in Agra? There must be some hidden agenda otherwise why should he deprive himself of the privileges that would come with being Maham Anga's son? His persistent efforts in casting a doubt on you also struck me as odd. Finally he made a blunder by mentioning about Mehrunissa Begum. He wanted to show me how intimate he was with Hasan.

Unfortunately that information sealed his fate and also that of Mehrunissa Begum. I asked him to visit the Begum's house himself and get some information about her last tryst with Hasan. But what I did not realise was that the Begum already knew about his real identity because Hasan had known it for quite some time. The Begum, grieving the loss of Hasan and suspecting Haider to be involved in it, made the mistake of revealing this fact to Haider and calling him a traitor. She realised the gravity of what she had done and was on the way to inform me when she was cowardly attacked by Haider who had become desperate for revenge now.

Mehrunissa's death alerted me to act sooner. I informed the Emperor and we caught Haider unaware. He had already lost his cool after committing the two murders and his arrest was the last straw. He spewed venom. He wanted to avenge the death of his brother Adham Khan. Before dying, Maham Anga had delivered him a letter, avowing him to kill the Emperor and avenge his brother's and mother's death. He is now in prison and awaits his sentence. I will always be guilty of not being able to save Mehrunissa's life. I was the one who had sent Haider to meet her.

✪✪✪✪✪✪

Twenty Six

FACE -OFF

Following Assad Khan's revelation the atmosphere in the chamber changed. The invisible tension was palpable to all the four occupants of the room. The softest sound in the background could be heard. The silence was so perceptible that Suraj and the inn-owner started feeling out of place.

Finally Assad Khan broke the silence. "You are guilty of spying on the Mughal Army but you are not guilty of murder. Your courage in staying behind and risking your life to foil Haider Khan's plan is worthy of praise. You have once again proved the Rajput valor of which the Emperor is an immense admirer. Honor before life. Consider it diplomatic immunity that we are allowing you to safely go back to Chittor."

For the first time since Suraj had entered the fort he relaxed his tense muscles. He felt lighter than he had in many days.

"The Emperor would like to meet you now", said Assad Khan.

"The Emperor has already met me", replied Suraj smiling.

"When?" uttered Assad Khan in surprise.

"Right here. I had a glimpse of the Emperor on my very first day in the fort. Stories of his love for disguises and moving incognito, especially when outside the fort have reached Mewar. I became suspicious when you did not introduce your stately escort to us. I observed him throughout and he appeared totally unperturbed by what was going on. The respect in your eyes and the command in his whenever you looked at him, finally confirmed my doubts that he was definitely the Emperor."

It was the Emperor who spoke up now.

"Your intelligence and presence of mind has always kept you one step ahead of us. Though you came from the enemy camp with the intention of spying on our army, your courage and valor has won my heart. I would also like to take this opportunities to welcome Rana Pratap Singh to Agra and extend my hospitality to you both."

Both Assad Khan and Suraj let out a sound of disbelief. The Emperor laughed out loud.

"As soon as you entered the fort with your friend I was struck by his extraordinary physique. My envoys who had met him had been especially impressed by it and always mentioned it to me. And suddenly it dawned on me that no other would dare to enter the fort of the enemy other than Pratap Singh. It was then that I thought of disguising myself as a common officer of the court and caught up with Assad Khan as he was proceeding to meet you."

Pratap Singh smiled for the first time since the conversation had started.

"A formidable foe is better than a cowardly friend. However, I have not come here to be your guest. Nor do I have any intention of entering into an alliance with you as the others who have blackened the name of the Rajputs forever. My only reason for coming here was to see that my friend Suraj whom I sent for my work leaves Agra unharmed."

"He will", replied the Emperor. "I am still unable to come to terms with the fact that on one hand you call me your enemy and on the other you go to such extents to save my life."

"You have already answered the question. The Suryavanshi Rajput places honor and truth above all else. We are the worshippers of Ekling Maharaj - Lord Shiva, the all pervading consciousness. "Satyam Shivam Sundaram." Shiva is truth and only truth is beautiful. The truth is that you and I are meant to meet in a war which will go down in history as a battle for honor. Nothing can change that." With these words Rana Pratap parted ways with the Mughal Emperor.

✪✪✪✪✪✪

Twenty Seven

THE LONG GOODBYE

Radha had lost all hope of meeting Suraj again. The fiery red ball called the sun was going down once again in the city of Agra. Radha thought how just a few days before, she was a carefree girl busy with her paintings. The past few days had changed her forever. She knew she would never be that carefree girl again.

"Radha, do not paint once the sun goes down. You'll strain your eyes in the light of the lantern. Your eyes have dark circles I have never seen before", her mother was shouting out her advice from the compound. Little did she know that Radha had hardly lifted the brush today. A feeling of intense longing had replaced all others. She did not know if Suraj was still in Agra and had no means of finding out either. She waited impatiently for the night, for it would bring with it the hope of meeting Suraj, however little.

Suraj and Pratap Singh had left the fort immediately and without any hindrance. Pratap was impatient to leave for Chittor. He did not want anyone in Agra to know that the Sarai at the city's end was being run under his supervision. He had never been seen at the Sarai except by his close confidantes.

"Suraj, we have to leave for Chittor without delay. I know for sure that we will be followed. We'll take advantage of the night to mislead those who try to follow us. I have had enough of the Mughals. Now I want to be back with my people. Father is also waiting anxiously for our return. We have to prepare the strategy for imminent war."

Suraj agreed. "Yes, the Emperor is very shrewd and I do not trust him when it comes to Rajputs. He has clearly decided to bring the Rajputana under the Mughal flag and he has been eyeing Mewar for long, though he might send another proposal of an alliance before actual war."

Rana Pratap nodded.

"You go ahead Pratap", replied Suraj. "I have one last unfinished business. I have to thank Radha one last time before leaving Agra."

"Hurry up the meeting. I will arrange for two horses for both of us and will meet you in the bazaar. The bazaar should be deserted by then."

The two parted ways. It was already dark. Suraj quickened his steps towards Radha's house. He could see the lamp burning in her room and her window wide open. Memories of the first night that he had climbed up the window flooded him. Within a heartbeat he was inside Radha's room and within another they were in each other's arms. Neither of them knew how long they stood like this. It was Suraj who first realized the passage of time by the sound of a horse trotting in the street below. He slowly let go of Radha's arms and looked into her eyes. Radha did not want to break the moment in which even the silence was talking to her.

"My work here is done. I am leaving Agra tonight. I know saying thank you again would sound empty. I also know that without you I would not have been able to see my people and city again."

Radha was at a loss for words. She asked the first question that came to her mind. "Did you meet the Emperor?" Suraj laughed. "Yes. Rather it was the Emperor who came to meet me."

Before long Suraj was telling about his meeting to Radha. Radha had little interest in the story now that Suraj was safe. She was trying to memorize his features and his voice as he spoke. There was the sound of hooves again in the street below. It was time to bid the final goodbye but Suraj could not find the heart to do so when all he wanted was to ask Radha to come with him.

"It's time for me to leave. I'll miss you Radha."

"Then don't go if you'll miss me", Radha replied and turned her face away knowing Suraj would leave any moment.

Suraj turned her back to face him. "Don't leave? I can't stay back in Agra Radha. It's impossible and improbable. I have been lucky this time because of you. This is our arch rival's territory. I came here to spy on the army. They all know this now. The only reason I'm alive is because you were able to convince the Emperor that I wanted to save his life.

"I know you cannot stay here but can't I come with you ?" whispered Radha without meaning what she said.

"Impossible" said Suraj firmly. Radha freed herself from Suraj and turned away. She did not want Suraj to see any of her tears that had started to well up. Suraj pulled her back.

"Radha, I'm a warrior. A close companion of Rana Pratap. My life is full of danger.We are preparing for a battle with the Mughals because soon thj e fort of Chittor will be attacked by them. My life will be spent more on the battlefields than with family. We have no future together. Don't make my good bye all the more difficult."

Radha swallowed her tears but could not speak yet.

Suraj sighed. "Can you leave Agra right now with me without your parents' consent?" Radha could still not speak.

"Say something Radha. Let me hear your voice again before leaving", said Suraj again.

"You know I can't do that. You can at least leave Agra with the promise that you'll come back to take me with you. Please don't try to get rid of me by talking about the dangers of your life. Did not danger bring us together?" replied Radha at last.

Suraj smiled and that gave Radha some relief and hope.

"I promise to come back Radha. Will you wait for me?"

Radha felt too much to say anything. She simply nodded her head.

"Then I promise that you'll have to wait but not too long. I'll come back for you and we'll sit by the Yamuna, this time in the light of the full moon before I finally take you away with me."

"You'll find me waiting whenever you return. Every full moon that will rise in Chittor will remind you of me waiting for you as I gaze at the moon here in Agra. Don't let too many full moons separate us by distance as you're already taking a part of me with you."

Suraj kissed her. "Let the full moon be the keeper of my promise."

With these words Suraj disappeared in the darkness and Radha started her new painting. That of a girl sitting by the banks of the Yamuna, beneath an old shady tree, with the full moon shining above and the moonlight dancing on the waters of Yamuna with its shimmer of eternal hope and love.

Glossary

Amma: Mother

Azan: Islamic call to worship recited at prescribed times of the day

Bazaar: Market place

Diwaane-e-Khaas: Hall of private audiences like courtiers and state guests.

Haveli: A large traditional house

Heera Kunwari: Hindu Rajput queen of Akbar , daughter of Raja Bihari Mal of Amber, sister of Bhagwan Dass. She is also known in history by other names such as Harkha Bai, Jodha Bai and Mariam-us-Zamani

Jabt: A revenue system applied on agricultural land under the Mughals.

Jama: A long coat popular during the Mughal period

Jazia: A tax imposed on non-Muslims during the Mughal rule

Kashi: Present day city of Varanasi

Kotwal: A police officer.

Mansabdar: A military unit within the administrative system of Mughals , introduced by Akbar.

Mashaal: A torch with a long stick and burning material at one end.

Mewar: A region in the south-central part of Rajasthan which includes present day districts like Bhilwara, Chittorgarh and Udaipur

Qumargah: Mughal's favourite style of hunting, involving a large army beating the animals to a central point

Rajput: Literal meaning is Son of a king, it covers various clans historically associated with warriorhood

Sarai: An inn, where people can stay cheaply for a short time

Suryavanshi: Belonging to the Sun Dynasty, a dynasty of ancient India

Tasvir Khana: Artistic studio

Gauri

Smriti Sekhar

978-81-936839-0-3 • Rs. 250 • 204 PP • 2018

Subject : Fiction

Size: 8 x 5.25 (Inches)

About the Book/Reviews:

There is always something consoling about a sunset. It is a strange time that dulls the harsh light of day, giving birth to night with all it's mystery at bay. It is magic that arrives when the crickets stridulate and when the moon has come to stay. And once the pink shafts have come alive, and marked a lover's song and all conscious has stalled to the dying of light, it is then you know, you made it. You survived another day. You made it to another dusk. You made it to Rumuk.

In a time and place, when girls weren't thought worthy of opinions, a certain girl develops a political one. Gauri is a fourteen year old who is "too rebellious for her own good" and takes onto herself the mammoth task of finding the truth behind her sister's disappearance. Embark on Gauri's journey with her to find each day reveal the mysteries of a village that will unravel your deepest fears and prodigious secrets. A page turner, be prepared to witness a game of nature that will leave you and Gauri deceived, yet wanting for more.

Smriti Shekhar is a student of History Hons. in Miranda House, Delhi University who holds the particular talent of breathing nature on pages. Coming from the town of Rishikesh, Uttarakhand, her proximity with the natural world has grown over the years and is greatly reflected in her writing.

With her book, Smriti hopes to transport the reader to the heights of the Uttarakhand region, only to explore it's depths and picture the events unfold in the book to their utter disbelief.

The Black Princess

Maggie Voysey Paun

978-81-9363-136-2 • Rs. 350 • 326 PP • 2018
Subject : Biographical Fiction
Size: 8 x 5.25 (Inches)

About the Book/Reviews:

Who is Mrs Helena Bennett and how did she come to live alone in the remote Sussex countryside?

Her neighbours know her as an eccentric old woman who roams the forest with her beloved dog, is generous to the poor, and smokes a hookah. They call her '*The Black Princess*', although she is not very dark-skinned nor of Royal birth.

It is spring 1853 when a chance visitor causes Helena to begin to recall her early life. Through her eyes the reader is transported to 1785 at the British Residency in Lucknow, India, a city renowned for its hybrid culture, the excesses of the ruling Nawab, and the avarice of some of the East India Company officers.

The Black Princess is based on a true story.

Maggie Voysey Paun has published stories about Indian children living in England and has written plays and adult novels which all have some connection with India. She has been married for many years to Rashmi and they have three sons and five grandchildren.

Her previous novel *Sacrifices* which is set in Africa, was published in 2016 by PublishNation and is also available as an e-book or in paperback from Amazon.com.

Ninety Days Escape from Uganda

Rashmi Paun

978-81-9363-139-3 • Rs. 450 • 396 PP • 2018
Subject : Biographical Fiction
Size: 8 x 5.25 (Inches)

About the Book/Reviews:

Ninety Days is a story about what life was like for Asians in Uganda before the President ordered them all to leave, and what happened afterwards as law and order broke down and people considered themselves lucky to escape unharmed.

In August 1972 President Idi Amin announced that God had come to him in a dream and told him to order citizens of Asian origin out of the country. He declared: 'If they are not out in Ninety days, they will soon see what happens to them!'

The story centres on the Hindu Mitani family whose biggest problems before the announcement are their elder son's choice of a Muslim wife, a sister's unhappy marriage and whether or not the community should spend its money on yet another religious shrine. But as the deadline approaches and there are beatings and imprisonments they, like their friends and neighbours, become increasingly desperate to find refuge in whichever country will take them, though they must flee more or less penniless and leave all their possessions behind.

Within ninety days, 70,000 members of what had been a close community many of whom were born in Uganda, were scattered across the world, mostly in the UK, Canada, India and the US, but some others across Europe and as far aflied as Australia and New Zealand.

Rashmi Paun grew up in Finja, Uganda. In 1972, when Amin made his announcement, Rashmi was already in London, studying for a doctorate in Physics, but his parents, family and friends were forced to flee from Amin's terror.